At Variance 3

Flash fiction and short stories

David R. Beshears

Greybeard Publishing
Washington State

Greybeard Publishing
P.O. Box 480
McCleary, WA 98557-0480

ISBN 978-1-947231-14-6 *(print edition)*

At Variance 3

Introduction

At Variance 3

Flash fiction and short stories, many of them adapted directly from short scripts, webseries scripts and pilot episode screenplays.

The narratives in these short stories follow as closely as possible the original screenplays. Genres include science fiction and fantasy

Note:
Several of these stories have appeared in other collections and magazines.

Table of Contents

089 - Sisters in Space
Episode 1 – "Awakening"
Claire and Amelia wake from cryo and find themselves eighty years into deep space with no idea how they got there.

105 - Sutherland House
Episode 1 – "Andover"
Matthew Sutherland battles a secret society. While its ultimate agenda remains uncertain, it is clear the Society is willing to go to extraordinary lengths to maintain its own security, and the safety and advancement of its members. In Episode One, Matthew investigates strange goings-on in a small northwest community while he and his daughter Jennifer come to grips with the death of Matthew's wife.

171 - Shadows from the Past
Short Stories Collection
Most of my earlier short stories have been lost, particularly those written using my old typewriter back before I had a computer, and more than a few written with only pencil and paper. But I did manage to hang onto a couple from way back when. Included here are a handful that I managed to find...

173 - Yesterday's Shadows
Written about 1975, heavy on TZ influence

183 - Reunions
First published in Necrology Magazine, Tales of Macabre

189 - Last Day at Sharp Park
Written in 1971, when I was fifteen years old.

197 - The Light in the Mist
A Victorian Fairie Tale (well, sort of...)

209 - Room
The assignment was to write a "white room" story...

Under an Alien Sky

Introduction

Survivors at a spaceship crash site struggle with the realization that they will not be going home, hope yet to complete their delivery.

Flash fiction story adapted from a 10 minute low-budget short script with three characters.

Under an Alien Sky

Lt. Margaret Jensen lifted the makeshift shovel she had fashioned from metal sheeting and stabbed it into the freshly overturned soil at the head of the grave. She straightened then, lifted her gaze outward to the stark, alien landscape of rust-colored dirt and rock. The pale silhouette of several moons hung low on the horizon of an orange-red sky.

The isolation was absolute.

Behind her was the wreckage of a small spacecraft, crew of three, and on this trip one passenger. She had been its young junior officer. She was in her late twenties, was dressed in a gray uniform of slacks and jacket. She wore a holster with pistol on her hip.

Captain Martinez appeared in the now warped access doorway of the wrecked spaceship. He stepped down the ramp and walked across the crash site to Jensen.

Martinez was in his sixties, had commanded this ship or others for more than twenty years. His complexion reflected his Hispanic lineage. His close-cropped hair was salt-and-pepper, more salt than pepper. He was dressed in a uniform similar to Jensen's, also wore a weapon on his hip. He was carrying a small daypack, the strap slung over one shoulder.

He stood beside his young lieutenant, looked briefly down at the grave before looking up and away from the site. He frowned, gave a barely perceptible nod.

"Thank you, Jensen," he said.

"Yes sir."

There was a long pause then, the heavy silence of the surrounding landscape pushing in on the crash site.

"He was a good man," said Martinez.

"Yes sir."

"A fine first officer."

Jensen gave a faint smile in acknowledgment. She looked back in the direction of the wreckage, then directly to Martinez.

Martinez glanced back, then again out behind the crash site.

"Dr. Brown is looking for whatever we might take with us."

"Yes sir." Jensen indicated the backpack that was slung over Martinez' shoulder. "Captain?"

Martinez shifted his shoulder, slipped more fully into the strap.

"Just a brief walkabout to get the lay of the land, Lieutenant," he said. "I should be back in an hour."

"Are you sure you should go out on your own, sir?"

Martinez raised a brow.

"Are you suggesting that we leave the good doctor all alone?" he asked.

"Sir?" Jensen thought on that a moment. "We should all go together, sir."

Martinez continued looking out across the barren landscape, ignored her comment.

"I'd like to get a better idea of where we are," he said. "We don't want to go out there blind."

"Yes sir."

They both fell silent again. Captain Martinez looked down at the final resting place of his second in command.

"It could have been worse, Jensen," he said. "Considering their technology, it could have been a whole lot worse."

"They did shoot us down, Captain. We crashed in the middle of the starkest alien landscape I've ever seen." She gave an apologetic look. "Sir."

"Of course, Lieutenant," he said, the hint of a thin grin. He looked from her then, looked up at the orange-red sky. "No sign of them. Nothing but quiet."

Jensen followed her captain's gaze. For the moment, the sky was empty of alien ships.

Captain Martinez shifted the backpack strap over his shoulder.

"I'm off then," he said. "Back in an hour. Be ready."

He started away, stepping around the grave.

Jensen spoke to his receding figure.

"Yes sir."

She looked again to the sky overhead, then solemnly to the grave before her.

Lt. Jensen entered the ship, looked across at the figure of Dr. Brown; he was huddled over a pile of equipment and other debris, sorting through it in his search of usable items.

Dr. Brown was in sixties, probably could have passed for early fifties in spite of having the look of a father figure. His uniform was similar to Jensen and Martinez' but of a slightly different gray. He wore no weapon.

The room was in disarray: twisted metal panels, seats askew on their pedestals, equipment and containers scattered about.

Brown looked up at Jensen before returning to his burrowing among the debris.

"Lieutenant," he said absently.

"Dr. Brown," said Jensen. "Anything of use?"

Brown indicated the two small daypacks sitting nearby.

"A few odds and ends; medical supplies, mostly." He continued his searching. "Sorry about Stevens. He seemed a decent sort. Are you all right?"

"I'll be fine," said Jensen.

Brown looked up from the debris, looked about the ship.

"Heck of a job, Lieutenant," he said. "Getting us to the ground in one piece."

"This is one piece?"

"I fully expected us to be scattered across several miles of alien scenery." He stood up then, gave an awkward stretch and sighed. "Some nice flying."

"More controlled falling."

A thin grin from Dr. Brown.

"As you wish." He grew thoughtful. "Were we in the wrong place at the wrong time?"

"We've made this run a dozen times. They've left us alone till now." She gave Dr. Brown a questioning look. "It could have been the package we were delivering."

"You mean me?" asked Dr. Brown. "Nothing special about me. I'm not that popular."

"Right..." Jensen let the word hang in the air a long time. "Half a hundred years, we still don't know what sets 'em off."

Dr. Brown reached down and picked up the daypacks, each barely a third full. He handed one of them to Jensen. He gave a playful wink.

"The study of the alien mind, Lt. Jensen. Kinda' my field, you know."

"Yeah, well, I expect you'll be late for your duty assignment."

Jensen turned her head then, looked up and to one side. She heard something...

The sound grew louder. The low drumming hum of an aircraft, and it was approaching.

Brown looked at the lieutenant.

"Ours or theirs?" he asked.

"One of theirs. Traveling low," said Jensen. She stepped back to the access door, stood in in the twisted opening of the spacecraft. She looked overhead, the sound of the alien ship fading. It left a hollow silence behind.

She stepped carefully down the ramp, carrying her daypack by its straps. Dr. Brown came out of the ship and stood beside her. He gave only a quick glance above before looking about the crash site. He silently noted the nearby grave.

"Any sign of the captain?" he asked.

"He hasn't been gone that long," said Jensen.

"Perhaps, but..." he said, looking up at the orange sky.

Jensen followed the direction of Brown's gaze, then looked in the direction that Martinez had taken.

"Yes. I know," she said.

"They know where we are."

Jensen looked again to Dr. Brown, again away from the site. "Uh, huh."

"Yes? So?"

"We have time," Jensen said in a sigh. "I expect..."

Captain Martinez approached the crash site from the back side of the spaceship wreckage. He walked around the ship, saw Dr. Brown and Lt. Jensen standing near Lt. Stevens' grave. They turned at his approach.

"Captain Martinez," said Dr. Brown. "Welcome home."

"Thank you, Dr. Brown."

"What'd you find?"

Captain Martinez put on a dark frown. "I made a circuitous route some distance around this location. Unfortunately..."

"One direction as bad as another?" asked Lt. Jensen.

"The top of that rise, helluva view," said the captain, nodding outward. "Saw nothing. Nothing out there, any direction, as far as I could see."

Dr. Brown looked to the rise that Martinez indicated, looked back to the captain.

"What do you suggest, Captain?"

Captain Martinez looked pointedly at Lt. Jensen for comment. She thought a moment on what he wanted from her, then nodded.

"They have our location," she stated. "We can expect them at any time."

"Our exposure out there would be absolute," Martinez concluded, directing his attention to them both. "And it is at least a three day hike."

Dr. Brown realized... "You're not suggesting that we—"

"We will make our stand here."

"What stand, Captain? They will attack from the sky."

"I do not believe so," said Martinez. "Their earlier attack on us was meant to bring us down, not destroy us."

"Captain?" Jensen started. "Are you saying they want to take us alive?"

"Not all of us."

Lt. Jensen looked from her captain to Dr. Brown, slowly back to Martinez.

"Our package," she said matter-of-factly.

Jensen and Captain Martinez both turned to Dr. Brown.

"Me?" he asked, startled. "But I'm not—"

"Of course you are," said Martinez. "Your expertise is a threat to them."

"By your argument, wouldn't they want me, you know, gone?"

"They want to know what you know," said Lt. Jensen.

Captain Martinez gave a humorless grin.

"After which you will be, as you say, gone."

The three stood silent for a few moments. Lt. Jensen gave Brown a sympathetic look. He tried and failed to give her a smile in return. He looked away.

"I see," he said. He turned away then, moved across the clearing. He sat on the edge of the ship's ramp. He looked up into the sky, back to his companions. He indicated the weapons on their hips.

"Those aren't going to do it, are they?" he asked.

"No," said Martinez.

"Not for very long," agreed Jensen.

"Then what are we going to do?"

"As I said, Dr. Brown," said Captain Martinez. "We make our stand."

"A thirty second stand..."

"Maybe a minute," said Lt. Jensen, shrugging."

"And then?"

"And then things get messy," she answered.

Dr. Brown gave a dark sigh.

"I don't like messy."

Captain Martinez looked thoughtfully down at the grave of his first officer, studied it. He spoke then over his shoulder.

"How long can you hold your breath, Dr. Brown?"

"Captain?" Brown asked uncertainly.

Martinez looked out then, indicated the distant horizon.

"Doctor... the outpost is about three days' hike. That way."

"I don't understand." Brown stood up slowly.

Martinez turned and looked to Lt. Jensen.

"Our package will reach its destination, Lieutenant."

"Sir?" she asked. She hadn't quite figured it out.

Martinez looked away, frowned and took a long, deep breath. He nodded slowly.

"Yes."

Captain Martinez and Lt. Jensen were standing in the center of the crash site. They wore solemn expressions as they looked outward, at the sky just above the horizon.

The very faint, low hum of alien aircraft was still far off.

Behind Martinez and Jensen: two graves, one alongside the other. The tip of a breathing tube was poking up just above the surface of the dirt mound of the newest grave.

The sound of the aircraft grew steadily louder.

"Here they come, sir." Jensen rested a hand on the butt of her weapon.

Martinez folded his arms across his chest. "Stand tall, Lieutenant Jensen."

"Not a problem, sir."

"Good." He gave a brief glance to the graves. "Not long to wait, Doctor."

The sound grew steadily louder. The alien craft were near.

A thin cloud of billowing dust began to roll over and past Captain Martinez and Lieutenant Jensen. The low hum of the descending alien craft shifted to a quiet drone.

The alien ship landed.

Captain Martinez unfolded his arms, reached down and took hold of the handle of his weapon.

He gave his junior officer a smile and a wink.

End.

Family Alone

Introduction

A family preparing for a camping trip come to realize they are alone in the world.

Flash fiction short story adapted from the first episode of a seven episode webseries in which a family explores a world suddenly devoid of people in search of an answer.

Family Alone

It was early morning, an hour after dawn. The middle-class neighborhood was well-groomed, with manicured lawns and shrubs. Family sedans and minivans were parked in clean, concrete driveways.

The street was quiet.

The Sullivan home was midway along the street. A wooden plaque on the front of the house displayed their name.

Dad was packing the back of the family SUV with camping equipment. Alan Sullivan was in his mid-thirties, medium build, with bushy hair. He was dressed in khaki pants and shirt, looked ready for a family camping weekend.

His wife Vickie came out of the house with a small ice chest and a thermos. Her hair was pulled back in a ponytail, and she was dressed in comfortable slacks and a long-sleeved shirt.

She handed the ice chest and thermos to Alan as she looked about the neighborhood.

"Sure is quiet this morning," she said.

Alan straightened up, stretched as he glanced briefly up and down the street.

He returned to his packing. "It's still early," he said.

"Not that early." Vickie took a step away from the back of their car, looked up the street. She spoke over her shoulder. "Spooky."

"Enjoy it while you can, Vickie," said Alan. "If only the campground was this quiet."

Vickie folded her arms, looked back to Alan, again up and down the empty street.

"It'll be fine, Alan. It's not a holiday."

"Yeah, yeah... your mother ready?"

"I tried calling a bit ago. No answer."

Alan stepped back from the vehicle.

"Okay, now that's spooky," he said snidely.

"Alan..." Vickie grumbled. Her mother had been looking forward to this camping trip for weeks. "She'll be waiting on her front porch."

She looked back toward their house as Connor came out of the house and absently followed the front walk toward the driveway. Connor was a skinny twelve year old with wild blond hair, was wearing a hoodie T-shirt. He looked frustrated, his focus on his smartphone.

"Connor," Vickie called out. "Where's your sister?"

Connor stopped several paces from his parents, his attention on his phone.

"I can't get a signal."

"Good," said Vickie. "Go get your sister."

"I should have a signal. I always have signal."

"Connor," said Dad, pointed toward the house. "Sister."

Connor groaned, turned around started back up the walk to the front door, his focus never leaving his phone.

Alan closed the back of the vehicle, moved around to the driver's side and opened the driver's side back door. He leaned in to adjust the packed gear behind the back seat.

Vickie stepped to the curb, looked curiously up and down the street. She wore the hint of concern.

"It's too quiet," she said quietly. She looked back to Alan. "Alan? Where is everyone?"

Alan closed the car door, rested a hand on the vehicle and looked up the street.

He said nothing.

"It's Saturday," said Vickie. "There should be kids playing outside."

"Seriously?" said Alan. "Have you met Connor?"

"Dads should be bringing out lawn mowers."

"Am I bringing out a lawn mower?" He looked toward their garage door. "Do we have a lawn mower?"

"You're not representative of my observation."

Connor came out of the house a second time, his sister trailing after him. Sophie was nine years old. She trudged absently down the walk, half asleep, pouting, rubbing at her cheek. She was dressed in light pants and a wrinkled T-shirt, her hair half-combed.

Alan gave a wicked grin.

"Oh my God, Vickie," he said slyly. "We're being attacked by zombies."

Vickie looked exasperated.

"Oh, Sophie... back in the house." She looked back to Alan. "Back in a minute. I'll lock up."

She turned Sophie around and guided her back to the front door.

Alan looked at Connor with a firm gaze.

"Connor," he said. "In the car."

Alan was behind the wheel, driving their family car along a quiet, empty street. Vickie, sitting in the passenger seat, watched the passing neighborhood in silence.

There was no traffic. There was no one outside. Windows were dark.

Connor was in the back seat, looking at his smartphone in silent frustration. Sophie was sleeping, beside her brother, held in place by her seatbelt.

Alan turned the vehicle onto another street. They traveled the empty neighborhood. No cars, no people, no lights.

Alan and Vickie looked briefly at one another.

Alan focused again on his driving.

Vickie looked out her side window, watched the homes and yards passing by.

She turned away then, reached for the radio in the dash and turned the knob with a click.

There was only static. She pushed the button half a dozen times to take the radio through the pre-set stations.

There was only static at each station.

She turned off the radio.

Alan looked side-glance at Vickie, keeping his focus on his driving.

"Call your mom," he said.

Vickie reached into her pocket and brought out her phone. She pressed the phone face several times and held the phone to her ear.

She waited, listened for an answer.

Alan glanced in her direction several times.

She gave up after half a minute, held her phone in front of her. She stared at, hung up. She put the phone back her pocket.

Alan turned the vehicle onto a main street, taking them out of the neighborhood.

There was no traffic on the main thoroughfare.

The family vehicle was parked in front of Grandma's rustic house, a large property bordered on three sides by trees, sitting along a long, narrow gravel road.

Alan opened the back of the vehicle and began making room for Grandma's gear.

Connor leaned against the side of the car, folded his arms. He wore a dark frown.

Vickie came out of the house. She walked across the lawn toward the car, wearing a concerned look.

"Mom's not here," she said, approaching Alan.

Alan straightened. He now looked concerned.

"You just spoke to her last night," he said. "Be ready first thing."

"Something's wrong, Alan. Her camping gear is in the front hall." She looked back toward to the house. "Something's wrong."

Alan looked to the house, then about them. Vickie's mother's house was isolated, alone on this gravel road.

"Yeah... yeah." He looked thoughtful. "But... she wouldn't just leave. She would have called."

"If she was able."

"Then... someone... someone would have called." Alan turned to look directly at Vickie. "No note?"

"Alan," Vickie said sharply, exasperated. "That's something I would have mentioned."

"Right," he said, absently. "Right."

Connor, still leaning against the side of the car, tightened his folded arms. His frown hardened.

"There's no one left," he said. "There's no one out there."

"Connor," Alan sighed.

"Grandma's gone. They're all gone."

"Connor," Alan said again, more precisely.

Alan and Vickie exchanged apprehensive looks.

Vickie looked then to Connor, back to Alan.

"Maybe not, you know, what he said..." she started. "You tell me... what's going on?"

"Vickie. You can't be thinking—"

"You tell me."

Alan had no answer to that.

Connor tiredly held up his phone, spoke without looking at Mom and Dad.

"No signal..." he said matter-of-factly.

Vickie ignored Connor, spoke to her husband in an insistent, hushed tone.

"Where is she, Alan?" she asked. "And the traffic? Where was the traffic? Not a single car."

Alan considered for a few moments. He closed the back of their vehicle then as he came to a decision.

"Let's check the hospital," he said.

Connor pushed off the vehicle, spoke absently as he moved to his car door.

"The big, empty building with empty rooms and empty beds..." he grumbled.

"Shut up, Connor," said Alan as he opened the driver's door. He slid in behind the steering wheel.

Vickie was the last one standing outside the vehicle, standing at the front passenger door. She looked anxiously up at her Mom's house, then about them with increasing concern.

The world was ethereally quiet... as if they were all alone.

She opened the car door. It creaked on its hinges.

The family vehicle turned around, started away from Grandma's house and down the gravel road. It stopped at the stop sign, turned left onto the main road and out of sight...

Leaving only the empty gravel road beneath the gray morning sky.

Fade out.
End episode one.

The Bench

Introduction

A man is sitting on a bench on the bank of a small lake. The last thing he remembers is dying. "No William. This is not heaven."

Flash fiction short story adapted from a six minute short script screenplay.

The Bench

The man was sitting all alone on a wooden bench on the bank of a small lake. The surface of the lake was glassy smooth. Much of the encircling shoreline was brush and tall trees. There was no movement, no sound. The solitude was striking. Man, bench and lake were alone in the world.

William was in his mid-forties. He wore simple pants and shirt, was clean and neat but for lightly tousled hair tucked behind his ears. His gaze was distant, his expression empty.

Time drifted slowly across the still landscape, seconds passing into minutes.

William slowly lifted his gaze, looked out across the lake... to a different time, and different world...

The bedroom was dimly lit, the curtains drawn. An elderly man lay in the bed, his head propped on several pillows. He didn't look well. He was awake, but appeared to be in the final moments of life. His face was drawn and gray.

It was William.

This William was in his eighties, but it was definitely William.

His wife Hanna and adult son were standing beside the bed. Both were distraught at the impending death of husband and father.

William lifted a shaky hand; his wife took it. William smiled weakly.

"It was a good life, Hanna," he said.

Hanna struggled to fight back the tears. She nodded curtly.

"I love you, William."

William smiled again, too weak to answer. Hanna looked down at their clasped hands. William's hold slowly loosened.

William's eyes slowly closed.

The younger William was standing now at the water's edge, his back to the bench. He continued to gaze out across the lake.

Another man was sitting on the bench, calmly watching William.

George was in his forties. He had soft features; his expression was gentle, kind. His hands were resting on his lap, fingers intertwined. He wore a silken, open robe revealing silken trousers and shirt.

When he spoke, his voice was warm and pleasant.

"Nice view, eh William?"

William turned slowly about, looked to George. His expression changed gradually as he came back from some mental fog to the world in which he now found himself. He furrowed his brow, looked numbly about them, back then to George.

"What?" He asked distantly. He glanced about them again. "I was..." The words drifted.

George indicated the lake.

"One of favorite landscapes, this. Your landing."

"My..." William looked back to George, disoriented. "Is this heaven?"

"No, William." George wore a knowing smile. "Not heaven."

William nodded dully, stepped back to the bench. He turned about and sat down beside George.

"Where am I?" He looked directly at George. "Who are you? You know me. How do you know me?"

"Give it time, William. It will come."

William didn't let his gaze leave George. It darkened, sharpened. He waited. He wanted more.

George took a long breath.

"My name is George," he said. "I am here to ease your transition back to us."

"Back. I don't understand."

"As I said—"

"Yes, yes," William said impatiently. "It will come."

George nodded in response, looked out across the lake. They were quiet for a long time.

"If you were to transpose the family concept to our realm," George started then, "I might be your brother."

"Brother? We know each other?" William asked. "I know you?"

"You do."

William considered. "I see," he stated flatly.

George put on a thin grin.

"Not yet, but you will."

Long moments of silence pushed in on the two men. They sat quietly on the bench. William's expression slowly changed, his brow furrowing. His head tilted slightly.

He remembered something. He felt... *something*...

He stood, stepped again to the water's edge. He turned his head and looked over his shoulder to George.

"I..." it faded. William shook his head. It wasn't there. Not yet.

George stood and walked to stand beside William. He looked appreciatively at the surrounding landscape.

"This virtual landscape is yours," he said. "It is the landing that you created to make your returns easier."

"I do feel a connection to this place," said William.

George was silent now, continued looking outward.

William frowned again. He looked hesitantly down at the backs of his hands. He rubbed at the relatively smooth skin.

He lowered his hands and looked at George.

"I died, George. I was eighty-five years old. I am eighty-five years old." He looked away. "I died. And then I was here."

"And?" George urged, prompted.

"This isn't heaven," William stated.

"It is not."

"It is... a landing."

"<u>Your</u> landing, yes," said George. "A virtual landscape existing between your Earth world and our realm."

"Realm?"

George considered.

"Home," he said at last. "Our home."

"But... I remember my life. My whole life. My childhood. I remember Hanna, my wife. I remember my children."

"Yes. Earth World. A virtual world created by you—"

"—in my mind," William finished.

George shrugged. "Close enough."

William grew distant.

"My whole life. My family. A dream."

"More than a dream. Less than real," said George. He grew thoughtful then. "You are particularly fond of your Earth World."

"Then I've..." questioning.

"Many times," said George.

"I see," said William. "And you?"

A sly grin formed on George's face.

"My tastes differ somewhat from yours, William."

A long pause, then William's expression shifted again as he recalled...

"Ah yes," he said, smiling. "I remember."

The two stood side-by-side, taking in their surroundings.

George was patient, content to wait, quietly enjoying this landing of William's creation.

Some moment later, William gave a slight, confident nod.

"I believe I'm ready now, George. I'm ready to go home."

George took a step back, indicated a path behind the bench that led away from the lake.

"This way then, William," he said.

They stepped away from the lake and walked around the bench. George placed a gentle hand on William's shoulder.

"We look forward to hearing your tale," he said.

"That will take a while," said William.
"I certainly hope so, brother."

~ end

Annie's Plan
Episode 1
"Comes the Dawn"

Introduction

Two young women at a desert campsite, early morning. The plan didn't go quite as planned. Jen is not happy.

This is the flash fiction short story adaptation of the first five minute episode of a six episode webseries.

Webseries:

Jen and Annie are small-time grifters looking for a big score. Annie had a plan, a great plan. But something went wrong, and they find themselves abandoned in the desert, their target long gone. Jen is not happy...

Leaving their desert camp, they start across the desert, following after their target. They find signs at a small watering hole, and will confront him at a desert shack.

Annie's Plan – Episode 1 – "Comes the Dawn"

A two-person canvas tent stood stark against the backdrop of a flat desert landscape. The ground beneath was a hard crusty soil blanketed in a thin layer of sand. Scrub brush and cactus was scattered beyond the perimeter of the camp out to all horizons.

There were two folding chairs before a small fire pit a few yards in front of the closed tent. Small flickering flames rose above the stone circle; a metal camp coffee pot sat atop one of the stones.

Jen was sitting in one of chairs, her butt slid forward, her feet set apart to keep her in position. She was holding a coffee mug with both hands, the mug resting on her belly.

Jen was twenty eight, dressed in khaki pants and shirt, leather hiking boots. Her short hair was mostly hidden beneath a cap, leaving a few curls tucked behind her ears.

She was not a happy camper. She stared coldly at the tiny fire before her.

Behind her, one tent flap opened and Annie stepped out. She also wore khaki pants and shirt, the shirt not fully buttoned. She was barefoot, carried her boots.

She stepped around the empty chair and sat, dropping her boots in front of her. She brushed at her shoulder-length brown hair with one hand, ran her fingers through it.

Jen continued to stare into the fading flames, doing her best to ignore Annie.

Annie reached into her boots and pulled out thick, woolly socks. She put them on, then positioned one boot and slipped her foot into it. She hazarded one quick side-glance to Jen before positioning the other boot and sliding her other foot into it.

"Nice morning, eh Jen?" she asked cautiously. She began lacing up one boot.

"Yeah." Jen kept her focus on the flames. "Real nice."

"You, uh..." Annie started. "You were a bit restless last night."

Jen shifted about until she was sitting up straight. She took a sip of her coffee.

"Hope I didn't keep you up," she said. She didn't sound all that sincere. She watched Annie nervously lacing up her other boot.

"Not at all," said Annie. "You know me. Nothing will ever stand between me and my eight hours."

"Yeah. I know... beauty sleep."

Annie fanned the fingers of one hand before her face.

"And viola," she said uneasily.

"Uh, huh." Jen leaned forward and reached for the coffee pot. "Coffee? Annie?"

Annie quickly stood.

"I can do that, Jen."

"No." Jen stared Annie back into her seat. Her words were cold, precise. "Let me do it..."

Jen picked up the empty cup that was sitting beside the coffee pot. She blew the sand out of it and poured.

"Don't you worry about a thing, sweetie," she said. "You just sit and... you let me take care of everything."

Annie reached out and took to the filled cup, a nervous smile.

"Thanks," she said.

"Milk?" Jen looked from side to side. "Oh. I'm sorry. I'm afraid we don't have milk."

"This is fine." Annie took a quick sip. "Fine."

"I really wish we had milk," Jen said smoothly.

"No, it's all right."

"Perhaps with better planning," said Jen. "Next time, huh? Some folks just have the knack. Ya' know. They can see things coming from a mile away." She turned a gaze to Annie, held it a moment, let Annie think on it.

She continued then: "Like, you know... running out of milk, for instance."

Annie turned away from Jen's hard gaze. She looked out beyond the camp, looked to the desolation surrounding them.

"He's not coming back, is he?" she asked.

There was a long pause as Jen looked down at the ground beneath her feet. She looked up slowly, though not directly at Annie.

"You up for a hike, Annie?"

Annie gave a nervous chuckle.

"Something I said, then?"

Jen looked at Annie, looked away. She slid slowly back until she was half reclining.

"It's likely to get warm," she said. "Unlike the *coolness* of the morning."

"Things aren't so bad, really," said Annie. "Are they?"

"Oh, Annie. No, no…" Jen raised a finger and turned her head, put on a studious expression as if trying to recall something. She spoke precisely then. "Everything is perfect. Right?"

Annie stared down at her coffee cup.

"I'm really sorry, Jen."

Jen was incredulous.

"Excuse me?"

"I'm sorry. I'm really, really sorry." Annie withered under Jen's *'isn't there something more'* look. "I'm sorry I lost us the mark."

"Your plan, Annie," Jen said bitterly. "<u>Your</u> plan."

"I know."

"Another one of your frickin' plans."

"I said I'm sorry."

Jen sat stiffly forward, threw her arms out, fingers of both hands spread wide.

"Look where we are, Annie!"

Annie glanced left and right, then back to Annie, avoiding eye contact. Her expression was one of a reprimanded child.

"Jen," she said, hesitantly. "You're not planning on, ya' know, doing anything… bad… are you?"

"Oh, *my widdle snuggle bunny*," Jen said, sighing, faintly ominous. She reached down and picked up the coffee pot, weighed it, set it back down. "The last of the coffee, I'm afraid."

She sat back, let out another long sigh.

A slow fade then…

Jen and Annie sat quietly before the morning fire.

End episode one…

The Black Tower
Episode 1
The First Floor

Introduction

The First Floor:
This is the short story adaptation of the first episode screenplay of an eleven hour, eleven episode miniseries.

Series:
A team of scientists travels the eighty floors of a strange black tower, where each floor is an alternate world fraught with danger, striving to reach the top floor and the dark force behind the creation of the looming monolith.

Note: The short story adaptations of all eleven episodes are available in ebook and audiobook formats. The eleven episode collection is available in an omnibus edition in paperback and ebook.

The Black Tower – Episode 1

Prolog

The Quonset hut sat in the predawn shadow of the black obelisk-like skyscraper towering eighty stories high, surrounded by the dark silhouette of the city skyline. Everything gleamed from an overnight rain.

Staff Sergeant Miller stepped out of the hut and held the door open for the civilian. SSG Miller, in his early twenties, clean-cut and dressed in starched army fatigues, moved with a smooth self-assuredness.

In sharp contrast to Peter Asher. Asher was in his late thirties, wore loose, casual dress, untrimmed and unruly hair, and had a quiet, preoccupied look.

Miller moved out ahead and opened the rear door of the black sedan. Asher mumbled an unintelligible thank you before climbing in.

Asher watched from the back seat as they approached the massive, windowless tower. The jet-black walls of the structure, and the asphalt from which it rose, were wet from the rain. At the base, a lone door was illuminated by an industrial strength light mounted on a tall tripod set a short distance away.

The sedan came to a stop. Asher climbed out before Miller could get out and open the door for him. He took two steps and stopped, let his gaze rise slowly up the side of the awesome structure reaching up to the sky, just beginning to take on some early dawn color.

Miller pulled a small canvas knapsack from the trunk of the car and stepped up beside his charge. He indicated the door set into the side of the building.

"Sir?" he urged, then led Asher to the door. It opened as they approached, and Corporal Ramos stood in the opening.

Ramos' face showed more experience than his twenty three years would suggest. His fatigues weren't nearly as crisp as that of Miller's; no starch and a bit haggard.

He gave Miller a curt nod, who handed him Asher's bag.

Asher looked uncertainly at Ramos, then back to Miller.

"Thank you for everything, Sergeant," said Asher.

"My pleasure, Professor. Good luck to you."

Ramos slipped one strap of Asher's knapsack over his shoulder. "Professor Asher? We should get inside."

"Yes," said Asher. He looked again to the sergeant. "Well... thank you again."

Asher moved to the door and disappeared inside.

Miller gave Ramos a sharp look. "Take care of him, Ramos."

"Do my best, Sarge."

Miller watched the door ease closed, turned at the sound of another vehicle pulling up. It looked just like one he had used to bring his professor over.

A young man climbed out of the front passenger side, a young woman out of the rear passenger side.

The driver, another army sergeant, slid from behind the wheel and opened the left rear door. Elizabeth Owen slowly glided out, seemingly accustomed to be waited on. Once she was clear, the driver closed the door and moved to the rear of the sedan, opened the trunk.

Elizabeth Owen was in her mid-fifties. There was an in-charge bearing in her manner. She was calm in her direction, and fully expected every order to be carried out without question.

She waved a hand to her staff without taking her eyes off the building in front of her. "Get the bags," she stated.

Ray Do and Lisa Powell both moved to help the driver. Both were in their early thirties. They were clean, neat, sharp and intelligent. They were science wizards who found themselves spending as much time doing menial labor for their boss as they did working in their field.

Inside the tower, Ramos squeezed past Asher and led the way down the long, brightly lit corridor. As they walked, Asher took notice of his guide for the first time. The young soldier's manner appeared as tired as his clothes.

That didn't bode well.

They stepped out of the corridor onto a wide landing. It was enclosed on three sides, with the side directly opposite opening out onto a large, sunny expanse. The sky was an unfamiliar shade of red. Thick vegetation, twisted and alien, covered the landscape.

The landing was little more than a balcony positioned thirty feet above the rest of the first floor of the building. Amongst a small collection of cardboard boxes and an assortment of canvas bags and packs were four other soldiers.

Lt. Gordon Quinn was in his late twenties, medium height, a slim build but strong. He had the manner of a military man without the severe gung-ho cliché. He kept his hair trimmed but not close-cropped, his face clean-shaven, his uniform sharp but not necessarily crisp.

Sgt. Sara Costa, also in her late twenties, would rather use her brain than her brawn, yet still came across as fully capable of taking care of herself. She was strong willed, knew what she was doing and didn't need to prove herself to anyone.

PFC Raso and PFC Carmody each had the college-kid look about them, as if their plan was to quietly do their three years in the army, then get out and go back to school. They wore the military uniform, but it wasn't enough to make them look all that military.

At the moment, they were using machetes on vines that clung to the walls of the landing and were threatening to move down the access corridor that Asher and Ramos had just come through.

Several M4 Carbines were leaning against the wall, and beside these two holsters with side-arms. One of the demands had been no weapons, but they had brought them in anyway. Wasted effort, as it turned out. Firearms wouldn't fire in the tower. There was no logical reason for it, but such was the case; leave it to illogic to sort out.

Lt. Quinn and Sgt. Costa were standing at the edge of the landing. Costa gave a sharp nod and turned away as Asher approached. She followed a narrow trail down to the forested floor below.

Quinn waited until Asher was standing beside him before speaking, and then he kept his attention on the alien forest that was spread out before them.

"Professor Asher," he said calmly. "Welcome to the First Floor."

Chapter One

The clearing was twenty feet in diameter, with four trailheads opening to narrow paths leading away from it. It was encircled by alien vegetation that reached high and loomed menacing overhead; brush and twisted trees and vines of thick rope and triangular leaves, all threatening to push in and swallow up the clearing. The few streaks of light that managed to stream in had a reddish tint.

Wes Banister knelt over the lifeless body of Captain Carver, lying face up on the floor of thick mulch. Nearby, Susan Bautista tended to Nathaniel Church's injured arm. The three scientists were visibly worn down, with the much older Banister and Church in particular having seen better days.

Wes Banister was in his late sixties. Long gray hair encircled a balding top and a face with sharp features and crystal clear eyes.

Nathaniel Church was a black man a couple of years younger, graying at the temples and wrinkling about the eyes.

Susan Bautista was Wes Banister's assistant. She was thirty years old, average height and a couple of pounds overweight. Her hair and makeup were worn efficient. She had a quiet confidence that showed itself in her manner.

She did her job and left the bantering to the professors.

Banister sat back, rubbed his pale face with both hands and looked again at the body of Captain Carver.

"He's dead, Nate," he said, glanced for the hundredth time at the vegetation that surrounded the clearing.

Susan Bautista finished bandaging Church's arm, stood and looked at Banister and the dead man.

Church, glancing at the bandaging, mumbled almost incoherently.

"Thank you, Susan."

Susan nodded without looking back, turned away from the others and found a level spot to sit down.

Banister avoided looking at the dead military man. "So, then. What do we do now?"

"We keep moving," said Church.

"I'm not keen on continuing down that trail."

"Neither am I," said Church. "But we really have little choice. We're in as much danger here as on the trail."

Banister looked again at the surrounding vegetation.

"Perhaps so," he grumbled. "It seems quieter here, though... d'you notice?"

"Quite peaceful," Church said with more than a hint of quiet sarcasm.

They both looked questioningly at Susan.

"The only safe place is back at the landing," she said.

"She's right, of course," said Banister.

"She usually is." Church positioned himself to stand, and Susan scrambled to her feet and started towards him.

"Let me help you, Doctor." She held onto his uninjured arm and helped him to his feet.

"Thank you, Susan."

"Yes," Banister said snidely. "Do bring the old man along, Susan." He picked up the machete that was lying alongside the captain and started toward the trailhead. He paused then, looked back at the body. "I'm not comfortable leaving Captain Carver like this."

Church gave a low grunt. "We certainly can't take him with us."

"No. No, of course not."

"We'll send someone back for him, Doctor," said Susan.

"Yes, of course." Banister turned back to the trailhead. "I'll take the lead for a while."

Asher stood at the edge of landing, mesmerized by the scene. From the landing, the terrain fell quickly away, the floor taking the shape of a large bowl. To all appearances, there were no walls and there was no ceiling.

There was a faint shimmer where walls and ceiling should have been.

Something was there. And yet, there wasn't.

He could hear Sgt. Costa behind him, at the back of the landing, directing the two privates, Raso and Carmody. She had them once again hacking away at the vines. They were complaining, again, but it was little more than background noise to Asher.

He saw movement below, and a moment later Lt. Quinn appeared from one of the side trails. He stepped past a small, thick mass of short brush and started down what Asher had been told was the main trail.

He was startled at the sound of a woman's voice, turned to see Elizabeth Owen following Corporal Ramos out of the access tunnel. He missed what she had said, but it had the sound of an order to her staff. Asher recognized the young man as her assistant, though he couldn't remember his name. The young woman with them must have been a fairly recent addition.

Ramos set down a bag he was carrying, looked quickly about the landing, and started in Asher's direction.

"Corporal," said Asher, turning back towards the floor.

"Professor." Ramos looked down at the trailheads. "The lieutenant out on the floor?"

"Said he'd be back in a few minutes."

Ramos nodded, scanned the floor again. "Extraordinary, isn't it?"

"It certainly is."

"Nothing can quite prepare you for it."

Asher glanced up at what should have been the ceiling. "Eighty floors."

"So the experts say." Ramos' gaze continually returned to the main trail. "The lieutenant is starting to worry. They should have been back by now."

Asher only nodded in reply.

"Do you know them, Professor?"

"Only by reputation." Asher indicated the floor. "How long have they been gone?"

"Almost a day. Captain Carver took them out."

Lt. Quinn appeared at the trailhead, walked steadily up to the base and climbed the rise toward the landing.

Ramos patiently waited, and Lt. Quinn spoke up just as he reached the landing.

"Yes, Corporal?"

"The last of 'em sir," he said, indicating the group he had just brought in. There were no salutes. This was a conscious decision. No sense putting a big sign over Lt. Quinn's head reading 'shoot me first'.

"Thank you." Quinn looked briefly at the people scattered about the landing, then back behind him at the floor. "Take Carmody and Raso down the main trail. Listen up for the Captain."

Ramos gave a terse nod and went to get the privates. Lt. Quinn waited until they were starting back across the landing before stepping towards the rest of the group.

"Folks?" he urged, moving into the center of the landing. "Gather 'round, please."

Elizabeth Owen sat on one of the boxes, warily eyeing the military man. Her assistants, Ray Do and Lisa Powell, stood behind her. They quietly watched and waited, looking to Quinn more like servants than assistants.

At least Professor Asher appeared to have an agreeable way. He moved to another box and sat down.

"My name is Lieutenant Quinn," the lieutenant started. "Captain Carver is out on the floor with the rest of the scientific staff assigned to this project. We expect them back at any time."

"Is the military to be in charge, Lieutenant?" Owen asked, somewhat accusingly.

"You have all been thoroughly briefed on the protocols, Dr. Owen. Captain Carver will be in overall command, but he will not be encroaching into the scientific aspects of the project."

"I should hope not."

"However, you will remain within the project parameters established by General Wong and Dr. Church. Captain Carver will step in should civilian activities endanger team personnel or threaten the goals of the mission."

"As was explained to us, Lieutenant," said Asher.

Owen looked from Quinn to Asher. "And what is your role here, Peter?" she asked. "Your name came up rather sketchily in the briefing that I was forced to endure."

"Professor Asher is an anthropologist, Dr. Owen," Quinn offered.

"I am fully aware of his credentials, Lieutenant," Owen said tersely. She looked back again at Asher, continued to speak to Quinn. "Our paths have crossed from time to time over the years. Peter is quite the respected figure in his field. Several fields in fact."

"Of course," said Quinn.

Owen turned then to look directly at Asher. "Of late, however, your activities have been, shall we say, hidden in the government shadow?"

"A few obscure projects, Elizabeth," said Asher. "Nothing mysterious. Nothing very important, really."

"Did those projects have anything to do with what you are doing here?"

"I have absolutely no idea what I'm doing here. I can only assume that it was believed my areas of expertise might prove useful."

"And well they might," said Lt. Quinn, jumping back in, eager to get the conversation back on track. "We have eighty floors to traverse, and, to be honest, we have no idea what we might find."

Owen turned her attention fully to Quinn. "And you, Lieutenant? What is it that you bring to the expedition?"

"Have no delusions, Dr. Owen," Quinn said curtly. "Your function here is to assist us in getting to the top floor. Anything that you learn along the way, other than what helps you in getting us there, is secondary. I'll be pleased as punch for you, but beyond that it won't mean a thing to me. I hope that I am clear on this."

"In typical grunt fashion, Lieutenant."

"As may be, ma'am. Now, if I might, I would like to get the preliminaries out of the way. Best we be prepared upon Captain Carver's return."

Elizabeth Owen didn't give Lt. Quinn the benefit of a response, leaving Asher to step back in.

"Please, Lt. Quinn," he stated quietly.

"Thank you, Professor," Quinn nodded to Asher, then spoke again to the group. "This landing will serve as our first floor base camp. It is from here that we will conduct our search for an access to the second floor."

Lisa Powell spoke up for the first time. "The floor can't be that large."

"Miss Powell," Quinn gave her a nod. "Welcome. As you have no doubt noticed, the inside dimensions of the tower do not appear to correspond to the outside dimensions."

"I assumed that was just illusion."

"As yet, we don't know how it is being done. The fact is, we have traveled much further than the exterior dimensions would suggest without reaching a wall."

"Will we be coming back to base camp each night?" asked Asher.

"Each--?" Elizabeth Owen looked from Asher to Quinn. "Surely you don't expect it to take that long to find the second floor?"

"It could, ma'am."

"Or..." Asher calmly urged, "we would have people on the second floor by now."

Quinn slowly nodded in agreement before continuing. "Each floor's base camp will serve as the one permanent location that you can count on. If we become separated, you return to base."

He indicated a row of olive-drab knapsacks that were lined up along one wall.

"We've prepared a small backpack for each of you containing basic supplies. There should be enough room remaining to accommodate what additional personal gear and equipment you may have brought with you."

"No, not nearly enough," said Owen. She could see that the pack was already nearly full.

"You were advised to bring in only what you considered absolutely necessary."

"I did."

"Yes, well, I am very sorry, but you may have to leave one or two things behind. Given the opportunity, once on the next floor, we'll return to the landing, retrieve what we can."

Corporal Ramos led Carmody and Raso along the main trail. It was just wide enough for them to travel without having to push brush aside.

"More of 'em," said Raso. "How many lab coats we gotta babysit on this op?"

"As many as they send in," said Carmody. "What's your problem?"

"Doesn't feel right."

Carmody smirked. "Of course it doesn't feel right. It's alien. It's gonna feel alien."

"I don't like it. I don't like any of it."

Ramos spoke over his shoulder without looking back. "It's not our place to like or not like it. Not the situation, or the civilians." He stopped then, having arrived at their first watch post. He turned stiffly about. "It doesn't matter to me one way or the other. I do my job, you do your job."

Raso frowned and grumbled under his breath.

"We do our job," said Ramos. He pointed sharply at a spot alongside the trail. "Plant it."

Raso took a long step and straightened.

"Plant it... oh, that's funny." He grimaced at Carmody. "Isn't it? I mean—" he indicated the vegetation around them. "Ya know..."

"No," she answered. "Not so much."

Raso called out to the retreating corporal. "Hey, what're we supposed to do if we see something? Throw a stick at it?"

Ramos spoke over his shoulder.

"Cry like a little girl. I'll hear ya' and come running." Ramos did feel a bit naked without a big, bad gun, but he wasn't going to let on to these guys. Firearms were useless in here, so they would have to make do. Deal with it.

To all appearances, it looked like dusk out on the floor. The reddish tint had turned to gray. Asher and Owen sat on the edge of the landing, feet hanging over the lip.

Animal sounds came from somewhere in the distance, crow-like yet more predatory, more menacing.

Asher could see Sgt. Costa standing watch along the left side trail. Looking directly ahead toward the main trail, he saw Lee Raso. The young private looked restless. He looked up toward the landing, in Asher's direction. He lifted a hand wiggled his fingers jovially.

Asher smiled good-naturedly, waved back. He continued watching the man as he spoke to Owen.

"According to Quinn, this is about as dark as it gets." He glanced up at the ceiling, which had now taken on the appearance of an early evening sky. "It lasts about eight hours, then daylight... or... whatever. The full cycle is about twenty four hours."

"Hmm."

"That might mean something."

"The man is a Neanderthal."

"Oh, Elizabeth," Asher smiled. "You've dealt with a lot worse."

"Hmm."

"Quinn's a pussycat."

"Well," she said, grudgingly. "Perhaps."

The animal sounds, which had been distant and very much in the background, were suddenly very near. Down below, Lee Raso was at full alert.

Asher spoke as calmly as he could. "The recon teams reported finding no animal life."

"They were mistaken."

"Apparently."

The world calmed, grew quiet again. Down below, it took Lee Raso a few more seconds to let the tension subside. Over at the side trail, Sgt. Costa seemed unconcerned, her focus on being ready in case the away team needed help.

Hearing the sound of metal plates and spoons clattering together, Asher looked back over his shoulder. Elizabeth's assistants were near the back of the landing.

He remembered the young man's name then.

"I'd have thought Ray would be out on his own by now."

"My magnetic personality," said Owen, not bothering to turn around. If something made an appearance out on the floor, she didn't want to miss it.

Asher gave a polite chuckle. "I can see that. Really." He turned back around. "He's been with you... ten years? The Janus Project?"

"Don't recall," she stated flatly. "He's doing all right for himself."

"I know you manage to get the plum projects, but I'm surprised that's enough for him. Let's be honest, Liz... working in your professional shadow can't be easy."

"As you said, I do find the little gems that keep us all interested."

Asher accepted that. He gave a nod back over his shoulder. "What about her?"

"Lisa is bright enough, or I wouldn't keep her around. And she frees Ray from some of the more mundane tasks."

"Which in turn helps keep him around," said Asher. "How long will she be willing to do the grunt work?"

"That is what research assistants are for, Peter. It's what they do."

Ray Do came up to them carrying a plate of food. He handed it to Owen.

"Your dinner, Doctor," he said.

Owen gave Asher a conspiratorial grin and took the plate.

"Why thank you, Ray," she said, oozing sweetness. "So kind of you."

Ray wasn't quite able to completely hide his surprise, turned quickly to Asher.

"Would you like me to bring you something, Professor?"

Asher groaned loudly as he slowly climbed to his feet. "No... thank you, Ray. That's quite all right. I think I'll burn the two or three calories that it takes to fetch it for myself.

Susan Bautista led the way along the trail through the vegetation, Church and Banister following closely behind. She had the machete in hand, had to use it occasionally to clear the path. Alien, crow-like sounds pushed in from the vegetation.

One of the vines suddenly reached out to Susan. She hacked at it with the machete and the vine pulled back, screeching.

Banister placed a hand on Church's shoulder.

Church pushed it away in irritation. "Stop babying me, Banister."

"Well then keep up, you old fart."

The trail ended abruptly.

Susan stopped in her tracks, Church and Banister came up short behind her.

Susan looked back over her shoulder at them. "But... this is the trail. This is the main trail."

"Yes, my dear," said Banister. "It should have taken us all the way to the landing."

Church nodded irritably. "Yes, yes. It may well have been the main trail earlier, but now they have closed it off." He growled under his breath. "We'll just have to hack our way through."

"With no trail?" asked Banister.

"We have to."

"What about finding another way?"

"Oh, come on, Wes," Church said impatiently. "If they're blocking our path here, do you think they'll leave a way open somewhere else?"

"It's bad enough traveling an open trail. I dread the thought of tromping through the brush."

"Same here," said Susan.

"Yes, well," Church sighed. "We are all in total agreement on that point. However," he looked anxiously about them. "I for one do not intend to stay here to await their pleasure."

Banister took a few moments before offering grudging agreement.

"There really is no choice, is there?"

Church gave a curt nod and turned to Susan. "Susan? If you please?"

In answer, Susan Bautista turned and lifted up her machete, brought it down decisively and sliced through the alien vines.

The animal sounds grew suddenly very loud.

Chapter Two

Asher and Owen stood at the edge of the landing, from where they could watch as Sgt. Costa led Susan Bautista up from the overgrown left trail. Church and Banister were stumbling along right behind.

Lt. Quinn scrambled down from the landing to the floor, hurrying to help... and to find out why Captain Carver wasn't with them.

From the main trail came Raso, Carmody and Corporal Ramos.

As they came up nearer the landing, Asher could hear Susan speaking low to Costa, repeating herself and shaking her head from side to side. "Turned around somehow."

Once on the landing, Susan, Banister and Church were guided to a row of boxes serving double-duty as a bench. Someone shoved coffee cups into their hands as everyone gathered around to hear what had happened; all but Corporal Ramos, who hurried over to the radio to let those in the command center outside know that the team had returned, minus the captain.

The two elder scientists told of an attack by the very plants that made up the forests, of vines reaching in and twisting themselves about them, tightening themselves around their torsos and arms and legs.

And of strange dark shadows that flew about the clearing in which they fought.

Church set his coffee cup down on the ground between his feet, looked up at Lt. Quinn.

"I have no intention of letting Captain Carver's sacrifice go for naught," he stated flatly. "I'm going back out in the morning."

"That is not your decision to make, Doctor Church," said Quinn.

Church glanced in Ramos' direction. The corporal was speaking into the radio.

"General Wong understands the importance of this project," he said. "And the urgency."

"We all do, Doctor. You must also understand the importance of being properly prepared to take on this mission." At a signal from Ramos, Lt. Quinn excused himself and went to the radio.

Church turned to the others in the group, most of whom had arrived in the tower during the recent foray onto the floor. He acknowledged Professor Asher.

"Asher, isn't it?" he asked.

"Hello, Doctor Church."

Church indicated Banister. "That's my sidekick. Wes Banister. Nice enough fella, I guess."

Banister gave Asher a tired wave. Church then gave Elizabeth Owen a smile.

"It's been a while, Liz. How have you been?"

"Have I ever been less than magnificent?"

"Not that I can recall."

Owen took a step closer and sat beside Church. "Nate, tell me true. What are we facing out there?"

Banister snickered, and Church smiled thinly, looked at the group as a whole.

"On that subject," Church sighed, "There is a bit of disagreement."

"A bit," grumbled Banister.

Church slowly shook his head. "And as of now, I have to admit that I just don't know."

"Whoa..." Banister straightened. "Someone get my diary."

Church ignored his partner in crime. "There are entities out there. Shadows... with a physical presence."

Banister cut in. "The vegetation itself seems to exist with a purpose, whether its own, or that of some controlling force..." His words trailed off.

"The Adversary," Asher stated.

"That would appear to be the case," Church shrugged. "Or... it may all be the Adversary. Not controlled by, but actually be this... being."

Banister stared down into his half-empty coffee cup. "Whether of its own accord, or at the specific direction of this entity, the vegetation is at the very least acting at the behest of the Adversary."

"And these shadows?" asked Owen.

"I have no doubt they are creatures of the Adversary."

"Or," Church urged, "are manifestations of this being. As the vegetation itself may well be."

Asher was struggling with the whole idea. He scratched at an imaginary itch in his scalp. "But, either way, why bother going through all this—" he indicated the floor beyond the landing, "all *this*, just to kill a few helpless individuals?"

"I don't believe the intent is to kill us," said Banister.

"Could he be trying to prevent us from getting to top the floor?" Asher had been given to understand that this 'Adversary' had specifically directed them to go to the top floor. "I was told that he asked us to come."

Church agreed. "He was very insistent about it."

"This is a test," Banister said sharply.

Church waved a dismissive hand at Banister, but said nothing.

"For what purpose, I cannot fathom," Banister went on. "But we are very definitely being tested."

"Melodramatic anthropomorphizing of an extraterrestrial whose thought processes we cannot begin to understand."

Banister struggled to not look flustered, attempted to put himself into a lecturing mode.

"A being arrives in our midst in the most dramatic fashion and asks that we meet with it, and yet insists that we first traverse a series of obstacles before we are allowed an audience. Sir... we can safely postulate that we are being tested."

Church looked thoughtfully at his partner for several very long seconds, the others in the group looking on as silent observers.

Church finally, grudgingly, nodded in agreement. "Very well," he said softly. "As sensationalistic as you insist on making what should be a straightforward presentation, I will –concede- to your argument."

"I am humbled."

"As you should be."

Banister snorted. "It is also quite evident that this individual, by stating its name as 'Adversary', is intentionally establishing a confrontational tone to this test."

"This being is an alien," said Church. "The thought processes behind these requests are alien. Therefore, the reasoning behind the requests cannot be accurately determined."

Just when that was starting to sink in, everyone's attention shifted to Lt. Quinn as he returned from the radio.

"Okay, folks," he said firmly. "I suggest that you get what rest you can. We have a go for the expedition, despite recent events. We move out at true dawn."

Banister approached the landing's edge, half lost in thought. The world beyond the landing held what this bizarre landscape took for predawn. The night was never fully dark, the day never fully clear.

At hearing Asher's approach from behind him, he spoke without turning from the view. "Professor Asher... trouble sleeping?"

There was a flicker of reddish light across what should have been the east wall of the first floor.

"I've never needed much sleep," said Asher. "Not sure if that's a blessing or a curse."

"Savor every minute of your waking hours, my dear Professor. When you reach my age, you will come to realize they are the only things of any real value."

"I'm not so sure about that, Doctor Banister."

Banister raised a brow and looked askance at Asher, but said nothing. Asher grinned apologetically.

"Please, don't get me wrong," he said. "I do place a high value on what time I have in this life. But none of it would mean much without what I believe to be the one item of real worth."

"Oh? And what would that be, my young friend?"

"The pursuit of knowledge."

"Ah, yes... I have heard of your idealism."

"Idealism be damned. The thought of reaching the end of my life and realizing much too late that I had squandered what years I had been given... that is downright terrifying."

Banister nodded approvingly, spoke as if offering a toast.

"May you have many hours of life yet before you, Professor, all of which to be dedicated to seeking out wondrous truths and the discovery of great and profound knowledge."

"Thank you, Doctor." Asher's brow wrinkled. "I think."

They stood in silence for a few moments. From behind them came the soft sounds of people sleeping: steady breathing, shifting and turning bodies, and someone's light snoring.

From the floor came the hint of a breeze, its source unknown.

"And what of you and Doctor Church?" asked Asher. "Haven't you spent your lives seeking knowledge?"

"Knowledge be damned, sir. We seek fun."

"Ah... fun. I believe I've heard of it."

"The secret to our success is our dogged desire to enjoy whatever it is that we are doing at the moment. If we are bored, or if whatever we are working on just doesn't do it for us anymore, we drop it and find something else, something that keeps the life in our lives."

Asher indicated the scene before them. "I would say that you have certainly found that here."

"If we survive it," agreed Banister. "But that just adds a little kick and spice to the project, eh?"

"Is that where the fun comes in?"

Banister gave a noncommittal shrug, and after a few moments grew more thoughtful. "So, where were you when we plucked you out of your earthly existence and dropped you in here?"

"A little college in New Mexico. Research mostly, and doing a little teaching." He gave Banister a side-glance and subtle smile. "But you must know that. You did select the members of this expedition."

Banister gave a shrewd grin in return. "I may know a little of your background. And yes, I've read a few of your published papers." There was a polite pause, then. "I liked the voice that I heard calling out to me from behind the printed word."

Behind them, the sounds of sleep slowly morphed to the subtle sounds of waking. Banister gave a glance back over his shoulder, turned again to the floor covered in alien jungle. "Our fellow travelers awaken," Banister said with a hint of resignation. "I believe it is time to get ready."

The group marched slowly along the same trail that Banister, Church and Susan Bautista had traveled the day before. Each had an olive-drab backpack, several of them overstuffed, particularly those on the backs of Lt. Owen's assistants.

The military contingent led the way, with Carmody and Raso out in front, Lt. Quinn a few yards behind them.

An uneasy, eerie quiet lay over the group. Even Church and Banister's bantering had fallen to silence. What sounds there were seemed muffled.

Carmody and Raso reached a fork in the trail and stopped. Lt. Quinn looked questioningly back at Church, who looked about them uncertainly before turning to Susan.

Susan nodded to the left fork, looked about again, nodded again to the left. She finally shrugged, waved a hand to the left.

Good enough, thought Lt. Quinn, who turned back to Carmody and Raso, pointed to the left fork. *Civilians. Gotta love 'em.*

Two hours later they came into the clearing where they had left the body of Captain Carver. The body wasn't there.

Susan moved well into the clearing, noted the disturbed ground from the earlier conflict, and the spot where she had worked on Dr. Church's injury. She saw the few traces of blood where the body of Captain Carver had lain.

She gave the lieutenant an affirmative nod. Lt. Quinn in turn gave Carmody and Raso a silent order and they moved quickly to stand at two of the four trailheads.

Sgt. Costa and Cpl. Ramos came into the clearing behind the rest of the group. At seeing the situation, Costa pointed to the far trailhead and Ramos moved to position, leaving Costa to remain at the trailhead where they had entered.

"But why take the body?" asked Asher.

"Why any of this, Professor?" Lt. Quinn was at a loss.

Church and Banister joined them as Elizabeth Owen found a place to rest, her assistants beside her. Church spoke as he watched Susan kneel down near where Captain Carver's body had been.

"This is most definitely where—"

"Yes," stated Banister.

Asher shifted uncomfortably. "I would as soon not stay here."

"Yes," Banister repeated. He gave Church an inquisitive glance before indicating the far trailhead. "That way, wasn't it, Nate?" he asked.

"I believe so."

"That way, what?" asked Asher.

Church appeared embarrassed to bring it up, and Lt. Quinn finally answered.

"The captain thought he saw something," he said, looked to the elder scientists for verification. "Perhaps a ladder."

"Only for a moment, then it was gone," said Church. "Several hundred yards distant. I'm afraid no one else saw it."

"But something was there," said Banister.

"Yes," sighed Church. "The captain said that he saw two ladder rungs hanging in the open air. We looked for it, but it never reappeared."

Real or illusion, thought Asher. *As if either has any meaning in here...*

After a long, uncomfortable silence, Lt. Quinn indicated the trailhead that Church had pointed out. "Shall we?"

An empty trail winding its way through the alien forest...

The sound of muted voices in the distance.

The vines on either side of the trail trembled. Tendrils began to move. The vines began to slide.

Slowly at first, then in a sudden flash, the vegetation rushed in from either side.

The trail was closed.

Carmody and Raso came into view. They stopped. They turned to face the rest of the group as it closed in on them.

"Oh, great," said Elizabeth Owen.

"Everyone stay alert," said Lt. Quinn. This didn't feel right. He pointed sharply at Raso. "Keep an eye forward."

He studied their immediate surroundings. The trail here was fairly wide right up to where it no longer existed. Behind them, the trail wound around a sharp bend. Sgt. Costa brought up the rear, stood alert there at the bend.

He made eye contact with her. She gave a curt nod, half turned so as to watch the path they had just taken while still able to keep an eye on the group, some of whom had already begun to settle in for what looked to be a break.

Asher stepped over to stand beside Susan and Church.

"Did we make a wrong turn somewhere?"

Susan gave an uncertain shrug.

Church grumbled. "It is possible, of course. It all looks familiar, but things change out here."

"I'm fairly certain this is the path we took," said Susan. "I could be wrong. A forest trail is... a forest trail."

Church's comment from a moment ago finally registered with Asher.

"Closing one path, opening another? Are we being led somewhere?"

"If so, I see no pattern, no design or direction."

Lt. Quinn turned to face them, focused on Church. "This has the smell of a trap more than a guiding hand, Doctor."

"Perhaps. But again, to what purpose?"

Banister spoke from his seated spot nearby. "This is the Adversary's game, Nate. We have yet to puzzle out the rules."

Church had to agree, if only silently.

Lt. Quinn took the comment to where it led. "We've already lost the captain to whatever is out here, Doctor Banister. Or whatever it is that controls whatever it is that is out here. If we can't figure out these rules, I doubt very much that it will stop with Captain Carver."

"Quite," Banister said crisply.

"What do you suggest we do, Lieutenant?" asked Asher.

Yes, thought Quinn. *What do we do?*

He looked to Church. "You certain this is the right path?"

"Not absolutely certain, no." Church stood under Lt. Quinn's sharp gaze. "I agree with Susan. I believe this is the same path."

Decision time.

"Carmody! Raso!"

They turned to look at their lieutenant.

"Double back and see what you can find," he told them. "Back in twenty."

They dropped their backpacks, left their positions and started back through the group. Sgt. Costa waved a hand to Ramos to move forward and stand watch in place of Raso.

Lt. Quinn turned to the rest of the group. "Take twenty, but stay alert."

Susan found a small hillock to sit on. She dropped her pack to the ground, sat down, elbows on knees, hands clasped.

Asher followed her over, stood above her. "Doctor Bautista... mind if I join you?"

Susan indicated the empty spot beside her.

"Take a load off, Professor," she said. "Call me Susan."

Asher dropped down beside her. "Peter."

"Hello, Peter."

"Hello, Susan," Peter answered. "How are you holding up?"

She gave a halfhearted shrug and a faint smile.

"I've been involved in all this since the day this tower first appeared." A second halfhearted shrug. "But you... you must still be at the overwhelmed stage."

"That is an understatement."

"Hmm," she slowly nodded. "Yes. I know the feeling."

Across from them and a few yards further down the trail, Elizabeth Owen was grumbling under her breath. Ray Do was trying to comfort her as Lisa Powell watched with a hint of indifference.

Asher felt an odd sense of intrusion and turned his gaze away. Susan was looking in their direction as well, but wasn't really looking at them.

"You know," she began after a long pause, "back when Doctor Church was first trying to put a team together, somehow your name kept coming up."

"So I'm told," said Asher. "Not sure why. I'm not as engaging as all that."

"False modesty, Professor?"

"Not at all. My career has been very focused. I'm an anthropologist, and not much else."

"Anthropology has many subsets, and you seem to be involved in all of them."

Asher gave a humble shrug. "And you?" he asked.

"Not much to say. I've been with Dr. Banister a long time. What career I have, I owe to him."

"False modesty?"

"Not at all," she answered precisely. "I'm afraid I don't do very well with people. This personality quirk can have quite an unpleasant effect on one's career. Then I met Doctor Banister. He saw something in me, was willing to overlook my, um... social handicap?"

"You're doing fine right now."

"Give it time," Susan sighed. "It shouldn't take more than..."

Susan's sentence faded as she shifted slowly about to listen to something.

"What is it?" asked Asher.

"D'you hear that?"

Asher listened a moment, then shook his head. He turned fully around, listened more intently.

Slithering, rustling, scratching...

Barely audible at first, the sounds rose slowly up to where everyone could hear.

Suddenly, explosively, branches and vines rushed into the clearing from both sides of the trail, striking at the group, wrapping around them.

As suddenly then... several small shadows came out of the brush, hovered a moment, then quickly clambered on first one then another of the group, jumping from person to person, making it all the more difficult for the humans to free themselves from the vines. Each shadow was about eighteen inches in diameter, and changed shape as it moved.

Lt. Quinn managed to free himself and hurried over to help Banister, who was almost completely hidden beneath the shifting vegetation. He pulled steadily at the vines, had to fend off a thin branch that slapped ceaselessly at him as he worked.

He looked over at Sgt. Costa and Ramos, who both appeared about to free themselves.

"Get the others!" he called out. "Move them out now!"

Costa scrambled over to help Susan free Doctor Church. The two of them helped him to his feet and stumbled toward the head of the clearing, in the direction where the path should have been, had it still existed.

Lt. Quinn helped Banister to his feet, started toward the others.

"Do it!" he called out.

Sgt. Costa lifted up the machete and brought it down.

The vegetation screamed.

Chapter Three

The Quonset hut was small enough that it's curved, corrugated sheeting seemed to hover over those inside. The interior was cluttered with desks in the middle of the room, wooden tables along the walls.

Corporal Johansen, the young communications operator, sat before the table on which sat the aging olive drab radio. General Wong and his adjutant Captain Adamson stood behind the young soldier. The General had the radio receiver to his ear.

"Of course, Doctor Church," said the General, speaking into the mouthpiece. "Yes. Success is vital. But it will not come if the team isn't around to meet the challenge."

General Wong was an Asian man in sixties with short, salt-and-pepper hair. He was stout in stature, had broad shoulders, and a tough, grizzly gaze.

He stared at his adjutant as he listened to Doctor Church. Adamson was in his early forties, tall, slender yet strong, with a sure manner and crisp dress.

"Yes, yes," General Wong continued. "Absolutely. As I have already said to Lieutenant Quinn." He listened again, glanced at Captain Adamson again before letting his gaze drift to an empty space somewhere above the radio.

"I'm afraid Doctor Lake isn't here at the moment," he said.

As if on cue, Doctor Lake came into the command center, clearly agitated, with SSG Miller right behind him.

He approached General Wong, politely but curtly waving one hand for the phone. The middle-aged scientist was prim-and-proper in both manner and attire.

"Ah," said General Wong. "Doctor Church? Doctor Lake is here now. He just stepped in." He stepped aside and handed Doctor Lake the receiver.

"Church? This is Lake."

General Wong moved away from the radio, waited for Miller to follow him.

"What is it, Sergeant?"

"General... the door is gone."

General Wong gave the sergeant a long, reflective look.

"Say again," he stated flatly.

"The door into the structure is no longer there," said Miller. "Sir."

Over at the radio, Doctor Lake was telling Church that they were on their own.

General Wong looked carefully at the sergeant. After some brief internal evaluation, he looked over at his adjutant, who, as if on orders, moved to the radio and took the receiver from Doctor Lake.

"This is Adamson," he said. "Put Lieutenant Quinn on."

Lt. Quinn was speaking on the radio, Corporal Ramos standing beside him. Across the clearing, Dr. Church was mumbling animatedly to Asher, Banister and Elizabeth Owen. Further down the trail, Ray Do was examining a minor head wound on Lisa Powell, Sgt. Costa standing watch.

"I understand, General," said Quinn. "Yes, sir." He handed the receiver to Ramos and stepped away from the radio. "I need everyone to gather 'round," he urged. Some looked his way, several started moving slowly toward him. "Please. Everyone."

He caught Sgt. Costa's attention. She gave a curt nod in response, remained on watch.

"Well, you've all heard," he said to the group. "We're here to stay, at least until we get to the top floor and accomplish our mission."

There was an undercurrent of mumbling from the group, and Quinn patiently waited for it to die down before continuing.

"Because of the current situation, it is all the more critical that General Wong and his staff be kept up-to-date on our status, and fully informed of any findings."

"And if we lose communication?" Owen asked snidely. "As our host apparently does not want us to leave, he may not want us communicating with the outside world at all."

"A concern of the General as well, Doctor Owen," said Quinn. "However, so long as we do have communications, each team has been directed to make regular reports. I will be reporting to Captain Adamson every eight hours. Doctor

Church and his scientific team have been asked to contact Doctor Lake daily."

"Of course," Church acknowledged.

Quinn turned to Elizabeth Owen. "Doctor Owen, your research team is also being directed to provide daily reports to our science advisor." To Asher, then, "As have you, Professor."

Asher gave Quinn a silent acknowledgement, after which Quinn turned to the group as a whole.

"For the moment," he went on, "Make yourselves comfortable. Our missing team members can't be far off."

Owen gave him a dismissive look. "And just what would make you think that?"

Carmody and Raso entered a large clearing and stopped. The only exit was the way they had come in.

Off to their left, above and beyond the vegetation, was the occasional flickering of the wall. The ceiling overhead shimmered, just barely maintaining its illusion of sky.

"Another dead end," said Raso.

They both turned sharply at the sound of rustling brush behind them.

Their only way out had vanished. The vegetation had closed it off.

"Like I said," said Raso. *Dead end.*

As they turned back around, a tall shadow materialized in the center of the clearing directly in front of them, forming out of a slowly thickening, inky mist. After several seconds, it took on the size and shape of a human form, hidden in black, flowing shadow.

Adversary.

It remained little more than a flowing shadow; vaguely human form, about six feet tall.

Carmody and Raso each took a step back, but there was nowhere for them to go.

Small, black shadowy figures began appearing all about the clearing, each just under two feet tall. Their miniaturized human forms altered shaped as they moved, as black amoebas might, returning to a recognizable form only when they weren't in motion.

The figure of the Adversary remained unmoving, yet its form never stopped taking shape. It was as if the black of space was in fact made of flowing, smoky robes shifting in a slight breeze.

"I am... your host," it said. Its voice was smooth, gentle.

Carmody and Raso looked briefly at each other. Neither responded. Carmody looked cautiously at the dozen or so dark shadows that shifted around them.

"I look forward to welcoming you and your companions more formally once you reach the Main Hall." Adversary slowly and smoothly raised a hand, pointing upward with an extremely long, thin finger.

Carmody watched the arm lift up and then slowly lower, finally disappearing back into the flowing, smoky darkness.

"You should be speaking to the lieutenant," she said. "Or to the scientists. I'm just a soldier."

"What would be learned from that?"

Carmody and Raso looked at each other in confusion.

"I don't understand," Carmody said at last.

The shadow of the Adversary shifted and flowed, softened and flowed.

"Quite all right," it said.

Carmody and Raso instinctively moved apart, turning slightly. There was a strange, hollow airy sound, as if the Adversary was taking in a breath. Its black shape seemed to take on a more solid form, held it for several seconds, then returned to its more ethereal existence.

It lifted its arms out and away from its robes, looked studiously at its hands, at its extraordinarily long fingers. It rolled the fingers, and as it did the vegetation that surrounded the clearing rolled in a gentle wave.

"One of you will end existence here," it stated, very matter-of-factly.

"Now *that* I understand," said Raso. He took another step further from Carmody, ensuring two targets instead of one.

Carmody stood unmoving. "And what would be learned from that?" she asked.

"Much," Adversary said silkily.

The shadow entities dashed in and about the surrounding vegetation. The vegetation itself shuddered.

"Oh, crap," Raso said in a hushed whisper.

"The other will return to the others," said the Adversary. "To convey my words of salutation."

Sgt. Costa was standing watch at the far end of the clearing. Lt. Quinn and Church were in quiet conversation, the others dozing or simply resting.

The sudden sound of the cry of pain came from somewhere in the distance, shattering the quiet.

Sgt. Costa started toward the trailhead.

"Stand fast, Sergeant," said Lt. Quinn, his voice calm.

"But—"

"This group stays together." Lt. Quinn spoke slow and deliberate.

"Your pardon, Lieutenant. They need help."

All were on their feet now, most looking to Quinn for direction.

"I will not have people scattered all over the floor."

Costa looked ready to bolt, but held her position.

Asher spoke hesitantly, unsure whether he should step into the exchange between officer and enlisted. "So we go together," he said.

Sgt. Costa waited anxiously for the lieutenant to give her the go-ahead.

Quinn agreed. "Lead the way, Sergeant."

The false sky looked about to explode into dawn.

PFC Carmody stood at the ready. At her feet lay the lifeless body of PFC Raso.

The shadowy figures were gone. Adversary was gone.

Carmody was confused and determined and angry all at once.

She heard the rustling of brush behind her. She knew that the path had been cleared for her.

She could hear Sgt. Costa's voice off in the distance, calling out to her, calling out to Raso.

Chapter Four

The black sedan pulled up beside the Quonset hut and SSG Miller climbed out and opened the back door. General Wong stepped slowly out, looked over at the mysterious black tower. He gave a sharp nod to SSG Miller before walking stiffly to the wooden door of the command center.

Once inside, he waved Corporal Johansen down when the man started to stand to attention. Captain Adamson, standing at the coffee pot, poured a second cup and had it ready when the general reached him.

"It may have been to test us," he said, handing him the cup. "Or to observe our response."

The general's angry silence was visible. Adamson was uncertain whether to continue, but was desperate to fill the quiet void.

"This character considers this all to be entertainment, General," he went on. "A game, Doctor Banister called it. It watches us, plays with us... tests us."

"A gauntlet," General Wong said absently.

"The Adversary made it very clear. They must successfully traverse these floors in order to reach what it calls the Main Hall, on the top floor; where it will be waiting."

"Yes, well, we knew as much from its earlier blustering." The general gripped tightly to the coffee cup. He had yet to take a drink.

"No one else gets in, and no one gets out," said Adamson. "The people we have in there now is all we get."

"So it would seem."

"And this Adversary has no qualms about killing them, murdering them outright."

The General lifted his coffee to his lips, took a cautious sip, and looked over the rim of the cup.

"A game, Captain?" he asked.

"Sir?"

"A game."

"Yessir," Adamson said uncertainly.

The General took another sip. "A look at the rulebook would certainly be helpful."

§

For the moment, the vegetation appeared content to let them pass. The team traveled steadily, following what seemed to be the main trail, at least for now, across the floor. It wound like a lazy river through the alien landscape, but always in the same general direction.

Carmody stepped into the clearing, almost stumbling in before stopping abruptly.

A vine-covered wall spanned the opposite wall, no more than five or six steps ahead of her, the rungs of a metal ladder visible in the vegetation.

"This is it." Susan hurried past Carmody.

The rest of the group spilled into the clearing, Lt. Quinn using gestures to silently order his military contingent to stand alert. Asher and Owen approached the ladder mounted on the wall, with Church and Banister coming up calmly behind them.

A thick cloud hovered high above the small clearing, pushing against the wall. The top of the ladder disappeared into the cloud.

Church curled a brow. "Not exactly the way he described it, is it?"

"Perhaps not," said Banister. "But it's the captain's ladder, nonetheless."

Quinn allowed himself to look away from the vegetation that pushed in from the perimeter long enough to look at the ladder; content for the moment. His captain had been vindicated.

Asher jumped up onto the ladder and climbed twenty feet. The cloud was still above him. He looked back across the floor, climbed a few more rungs, looked about again curiously.

"It's there!" he called down, started hurriedly down the ladder. "It's right there!"

"What's there?" Owen asked irritably.

"The landing," Asher jumped down from the ladder. "Where we came in—it isn't more than a few hundred feet away."

Lt. Quinn was lost. "I don't under—"

"It's right beside us," Asher said insistently. "The landing is right there."

Most of the group had turned to look into the alien vegetation, thinking about the route that had brought them here. Church didn't need to.

"That would certainly be in keeping with our host's droll sense of wit," he stated quietly.

Owen looked away from encroaching vegetation and once again let her gaze rise slowly up the ladder.

"I never noticed that cloud," she said thoughtfully. "Not from the landing, not from anywhere."

Church followed where she was looking. "A ladder that appears for only a moment, that may or may not be there. A cloud that—"

Banister cut him off. "I'll bet you a sack of pennies that once you leave this clearing, that cloud can't be seen. It doesn't exist."

Owen was still trying to wrap her head around it. "But how the—"

"It really didn't become clear to me until Private Carmody described her meeting with the Adversary," said Banister. "I had mistakenly assumed this was part of the illusion of the floor."

"I don't understand, Doctor," said Quinn.

"Yes," grumbled Church. "What are you dribbling on about, Banister?"

"I was wrong, you see."

"Hallelujah," Church exaggeratedly fanned his hands in the air.

Banister chose to ignore him.

"We can expect each floor to maintain an illusion of being something other than simply a floor in the building, but I believe this floor's own unique aspect is its constantly changing features."

"And the little things," Susan thought aloud, "like a cloud that is visible from only one location."

"All quite disconcerting," Banister looked to Church. "And quite in keeping with our host's—*drollness*."

"I see," Church nodded. "You might just be onto something, Banister."

"Which is?" Lt. Quinn urged.

Church was looking carefully at his friend Banister. "This Adversary placed the shifting visage concept, and these other oddities, on the first floor, where we must also, simultaneously, come to terms with the concept of the interior of this tower appearing to be larger than the container itself." Church let the thought process itself. "Interesting," he mumbled at last.

"Be careful," Banister frowned. "You'll pop a brain cell."

"But the captain—" Susan started.

"Yes," Owen cut her off. "What about that?"

"The ladder was meant to be seen," said Banister. "At that moment, by Captain Carver."

"To draw us in," Church wondered.

"Possibly, though we really can't know that for certain." Banister breathed out heavily. "We'll need to gather more information."

Lt. Quinn was wondering how he could possibly get this group up through another seventy nine floors, when every floor was... *what?*

"You don't think the other floors will be like this?"

"I doubt it, Lieutenant," Banister said curtly. "More likely, each will be very different; each will have its own distinct properties. Whatever else we may find, the aspects that we are witnessing here may well be unique to this floor."

"Or not," said Church.

"Quite," said Banister. "Or not."

Asher was looking restless.

"Let's do this," he said, and reached out for the ladder.

Lt. Quinn placed a hand on his arm, looked over at his sergeant.

"Sergeant Costa? Lead the way, please."

Sgt. Costa shifted her backpack and approached the ladder. Asher stepped aside and she put one foot onto a rung, then the other onto the rung above. Behind her, the others in the group drifted slowly nearer. Each in turn started up.

§

They settled into an easy pace set by Sgt. Costa. Asher fell into the rhythm of Costa's boots, the sound they made as they slid onto the rungs just above his head. The cloud that enveloped them hid the rest of the group from his view, though he could hear their breathing, the soles of their boots sliding onto rungs, their shifting gear.

Elizabeth Owen's voice came from somewhere below.

"Anyone counting?"

"I started to," said Church. "Somewhat late I'm afraid. I gave it up."

"Jack and the bloody damn beanstalk," Owen grumbled.

Asher grinned, called up to Costa above him. "Call out if you see a castle, Sergeant."

"Yes sir." She apparently didn't get the joke.

It was another full minute before Sgt. Costa stopped her methodic step, boot to rung, boot to rung.

Asher waited.

Sgt. Costa's words drifted down to him. "We're here, Professor."

"We're at the top," Asher called down. He looked up again toward Sgt. Costa, saw only her boots and her legs. "What do you see, Sergeant?"

"It looks like a submarine hatch," she said. "You know... a wheel in the center."

"Go for it."

"You got it."

Again Asher waited. He thought he heard the sound of metal against metal, but he couldn't be sure.

Owen called out again from somewhere below. "What the hell is happening up there?"

"Ever the restless, eh, Elizabeth?" Church's voice. A few seconds later, he called up calmly. "So, Professor Asher... just what is going on?"

"She's opening the hatch now."

A moment's silence, then Church passed the word down.

"We are advancing, Doctor Owen. Our moment of glory awaits us."

Above Asher, the cloud thinned slightly. He could just make out Sgt. Costa's torso, arms reaching upward, the shadow of the round hatch.

She gave the wheel a final turn. She looked below her at the upturned face of Professor Asher.

"Okay," she sighed. "That's it, Professor... open it?"

"Nothing for us here, Sara."

"Yes, sir." Sgt. Costa turned her attention again to the hatch. "Onward and upward then."

She pushed up. The hatch lifted easily.

Sgt. Costa climbed up through a rusted hatchway and out onto the deck of an aging freighter.

The ship looked long abandoned; rust everywhere, dents in the wall of a small cabin behind her, the railing in front of her twisted out of shape.

Asher climbed up after her. The two of them moved apprehensively toward the railing.

The color of the sea was a strange dark green. A lime green sky hovered above it like a glowing shell. An overly large moon hung low on the horizon.

One by one, the others in the group climbed up through the hatch and onto the deck. Each moved numbly toward the rail. The hint of a warm breeze brushed their faces.

A long, serpentine creature rose above the surface of the sea a few hundred yards from the ship, slid slowly back beneath the gently rolling waves...

~ *end of episode one*

The Bridge Crew
Episode One
"Trial Run"

Introduction

"Trial Run" is a short story adaptation of the first episode screenplay of "The Bridge Crew", a six episode science fiction webseries with one set, five characters and minimal CGI. The entire series takes place on the bridge of an exploration starship with CGI displayed on the forward viewer, the five characters working at their assigned duty stations.

The first episode introduces the characters and the structure of the series as the starship is redirected from its initial shakedown cruise to instead recover a group of scientists before a star goes nova. They come across several suspicious, previously uncharted asteroid fields en route, and indications of a previously unknown alien race.

The episode sets the stage for the remaining five episodes of the webseries.

The Bridge Crew – Episode One – Trial Run

The starship's bridge was empty, dimly lit. It had five duty stations, one for each of the officers of the bridge crew. Each station had a built-in computer console. The captain's station, in the center of the oval-shaped room, had its own console station attached to an articulating arm.

There was a windowless door set in the back wall, a large view screen mounted on the front wall.

The overhead lighting activated as the rear door slid aside and Lieutenant Mike Saldana came onto the bridge. He was thirty two, slim, with a strong Hispanic appearance. He wore the official uniform of gray shirt and pants, the insignia of the lieutenant on his collar.

He sat at the communication station and put on his headset.

Lt. Saldana was the communications officer of the Explorer 3, Starcruiser Class, first generation design, exploration vehicle of the Earth Expeditionary Force. It had limited defensive capabilities and minimal weaponry.

The starship had just come off the production line, had yet to go on its first mission.

Captain Robert Smith came onto the bridge then; middle-aged Caucasian, tall, well-groomed, solid features but with a kind way about him.

Lt. Saldana looked up from his work station.

"Good morning, Captain."

"Good morning, Lieutenant." Captain Smith moved to the command station, pulled his work console to him. His monitor activated; he read the data that scrolled up the screen.

Lt. Jefferson Underhill came onto the bridge, went quickly to the engineering station. Underhill was forty years old, quite short, husky, with bushy brown hair. He maneuvered himself onto his seat and activated his work station. The light from the screen reflected on his face as he studied the data.

Captain Smith glanced briefly up and across to his engineer.

"Lieutenant Underhill," he said, casually.

"Captain Smith," said Underhill, looking side-glance, his focus on his console.

Commander Joan Browning and Lt. Commander Brenda Whitfield came onto the bridge together. Commander Browning was a middle-aged black woman with gray heavily sprinkled through her hair. She was the ship's first officer and its science officer. Lt. Commander Whitfield served as the navigation and tactical officer. She was thirty five, had a slim figure and slight features, kept her light hair trimmed short. She had a confident, self-assured manner.

Captain Smith looked up from his console and about the bridge.

"Good morning, everyone."

"Captain," Commander Browning stated flatly.

Whitfield had moved to the navigation station in front of the captain's station, slid now into position and activated her console.

"Sir," she stated.

Captain Smith turned now to face the ship's engineer.

"Lieutenant Underhill. Wake her up, please."

"Aye sir." Underhill worked his console. "All systems coming on line."

Captain Smith turned to Saldana.

"Lieutenant Saldana. Communications, if you please."

Saldana half turned from his station. "Comm systems active, Captain."

Captain Smith gave a thank you nod, faced forward. He looked side-glance to Commander Browning.

"How do we look, Commander?"

"All systems green, Captain," said Browning.

Saldana had a finger pressed against his earpiece. He listened for several moments, then turned to the captain. "Admiral Tanaka for you, sir."

"My station, Saldana. And put it on the forward viewer."

The image of Admiral Satoshi Tanaka appeared on the screen. He was Japanese, his gray hair well-trimmed. He had strong facial features, sharp clear eyes; admiral insignia was pinned to his collar.

"Admiral Tanaka," said Captain Smith. "Good morning, sir."

"Captain Smith." Admiral Tanaka gave a brief, abrupt nod. "I trust you and your crew are settling into your new digs."

"Yes, Admiral. Love that new spaceship smell."

"Wonderful. So glad you like it."

"Absolutely, Admiral. Can't wait to take it for a spin."

"Yes, yes." Admiral Tanaka hesitated. "Change in plans there, I'm afraid. The exploratory mission we had you scheduled for as your shakedown cruise has been shelved."

"Sir..."

"You will be going to Syratahn. You will locate a group of wayward scientists, get them off planet before their star goes nova."

"Not a problem, sir. Can do."

"The population of the planet was evacuated months ago, but we've had a team there studying the impending nova close up for more than a year. They were scheduled to return two weeks ago, and we have been unable to contact them."

"Yes sir. What kind of timeline are we looking at, Admiral?"

"Days."

"I see," said Captain Smith. "Best we get started then."

"Good luck, Bob; to you and your crew."

"Thank you, Admiral." Captain Smith waited for the admiral's image to vanish from the viewer, then spoke calmly to the navigation officer. "Lt. Commander Whitfield, take us out of orbit. Set course for Syratahn."

"Aye, sir." Whitfield initiated the sequence to take the ship out. On the forward viewer the planet drifted out of the display. "Leaving orbit. Course laid in for Syratahn."

"Speed L-3," said the captain.

"Aye, sir. Speed L-3," said Whitfield. The forward viewer display reflected the shift to light speed.

The bridge crew settled into their duties. The science officer, Commander Joan Browning, quietly studied the mission data that had been downloaded to her station. Engineering Officer Lieutenant Underhill monitored engines and ship's systems. Communications Officer Lieutenant Mike Saldana reviewed personnel data and Syratahn technology downloaded to his station. Navigation / Tactical Officer Lt. Commander Whitfield worked the keypad on her station, focused on her monitor as she occasionally glanced up at the forward viewer.

Captain Smith settled back into his command chair, pulled his work station around to study the data on the monitor.

A day and a half out...

Commander Browning noticed something on the console of her science station. She looked curiously at the display. She pressed a key.

All the more curious...

"Captain, we have unidentified targets ahead," she said. "Thousands of 'em; we're coming up on them fast."

"Helm, reduce speed." Captain Smith swiveled his chair around to look forward. "Take us to L-1."

"Aye, sir," said Whitfield. "Speed L-1."

Captain Smith shifted slightly to look again to Browning. "Commander Browning, do you have visual?"

"Not yet, sir. But readings show targets going out as far as my instruments reach."

"Asteroids?"

"Thousands of them."

Whitfield was working her keypad as she studied data on her monitor. "There is no record of an asteroid field in this sector, Captain."

"Record or no, we have one now." Captain Smith looked from Whitfield to Browning. "How long to go around it, Commander? At top speed?"

"I don't see where it ends," said Commander Browning. "I couldn't tell you."

"Right. Send your data to helm."

"Yes sir." Browning forwarded the data to the navigation station. As she did, her monitor flashed with new data of its own. She gave a quick glance. "I have visual now, Captain."

"Put it on the forward viewer."

A moment, then the viewer flickered and changed, displayed the asteroid field far in the distance; it was little more than flecks set against the black of space. The individual asteroids were set far apart, as was normal for an asteroid field.

Captain Smith shifted forward, furrowed his brow as he studied the display.

"Dead slow, helm."

"Aye sir," said Whitfield. "Dead slow."

Commander Browning looked up from her work station. "Still unable to identify its boundaries, Captain."

"Very well," said Captain Smith. "We have a star going nova at any time and a group of scientists that could probably use a lift. We'll have to go through."

"Sir?" said Browning, questioning.

"Give me another option."

"I don't have one."

"Right." Captain Smith turned forward, gave a nod to Whitfield. "Maintain your heading, Lt. Commander; ready tactical."

"Yes sir," said Whitfield and calmly shifted attention to a secondary keypad. Navigation and tactical was dual station on Starcruiser class exploration ships.

"Shoot anything that gets in our way," said Captain Smith.

"Aye sir."

The bridge fell quiet, each member of the crew silently working their stations. Captain Smith kept his attention on the forward viewer. Long moments passed as the viewer showed the steady approach of an asteroid.

Whitfield worked the tactical keypad, targeted and fired the ship's laser weapon. The asteroid disintegrated. Tiny remnants struck the ship's shields as the ship passed through the cloud.

"Shields holding," said Underhill from his engineering station.

The ship approached another asteroid. This was dealt with similarly to the first.

Whitfield adjusted course to avoid a third.

Several asteroids appeared in the display. Whitfield targeted one, tried to avoid another. It came upon them quickly. There was a powerful, physical jolt and a loud bang as the large asteroid hit the shield hard, the sound of the strike echoing throughout the bridge.

"Sorry, folks," said Whitfield.

Underhill noted the data displaying on his console.

"Minimal damage to the hull, automated repairs underway. Shields down fifteen percent," he said matter-of-factly. He looked directly at the captain. "Auto repair, shields, weapons... it's all taking power. More than anticipated."

"We need shields through the belt, Engineer. And weapons."

"Aye, and the ship needs a hull as well. It all takes energy. It all draws from the same energy."

"Will there be enough left in the power rods to get us to Syratahn?"

"It all depends on how many more strikes the shields have to absorb." He gave a nod in Whitfield's direction. "And how many more shots Tex over there has to take."

"Lt. Commander?" Captain Smith asked Whitfield.

"They're widely spaced, but we've a ways to go, Captain," said Whitfield. "There's no avoiding 'em all."

Captain Smith leaned back in his command chair. "Let us continue..."

"You got it, sir," said Whitfield.

The forward viewer displayed a large asteroid passing to ship's port. Directly ahead was only the black of space.

Commander Browning looked up from her monitor.

"Coming out of the asteroid field now, Captain," she said.

"Confirmed, Captain," said Whitfield from her navigation station. "We're clear."

Captain Smith gave a slow nod, looked from the viewer across to his engineer.

"How do we look power-wise, Underhill?"

"Reserves took a heck of a hit." Lt. Underhill was running calculations. It took another twenty seconds. He looked up from his monitor then, gave a half-shrug. "If we push remaining repairs to background, if we keep to L-2..."

Captain Smith turned to navigation. "Will that get us there in time?"

"I believe so, sir," said Whitfield.

"The calculations regarding the nova are not exact, Captain," said Commander Browning.

"Understood, Commander. We work with what we have." Captain Smith swiveled forward. "Get us there, Lt. Commander."

"Aye sir." Whitfield worked her keypad. "On our way."

Captain Smith settled back into his command chair, absently watched the forward viewer.

The bridge had been quiet for hours, the low hum sound of equipment and systems intruded upon only occasionally by a question or comment from one crew member to another, a simple answer from another in response.

The navigation officer alerted the bridge without looking up from her station.

"Approaching Syratahn," she said. "Dead ahead."

"Take us out of light, Lt. Commander," said Captain Smith.

"Aye, sir. Impulse."

The forward viewer showed the light shift. Moments later a planet appeared in the center of the display, still some distance out.

Engineer Underhill was monitoring the ship's energy levels.

"I'll need to do some additional calculations," he said. "But I think the power rods have enough left in 'em to get us to Amber 3."

"Thank you, Lieutenant," said Captain Smith. "Let me know when you have hard numbers."

At the communication station, Lieutenant Saldana received a message from the planet. He carefully listened before alerting the captain.

"I'm receiving a recorded message from the science station on the surface," he said.

"And?"

"Interference, difficult to hear," Saldana said, shaking his head. He lifted a hand, raised a finger, listened intently. He repeated then what was coming through his headset.

"Experiencing severe earthquakes... weather disturbances... not certain how long can hold out. Please help." Another shake of his head. "It repeats."

"See if you can contact them," said the captain.

"Attempting to do so," said Saldana.

Lt. Commander Whitfield alerted those on the bridge, "Coming up on the planet."

"Put us in orbit," Captain Smith stated.

"Initiating sequence." Whitfield worked her console, initiated orbit sequence.

All on the bridge watched the shifting display on the viewer. Half a minute later, Whitfield brushed keys on her work station.

"Safely in orbit," she said.

"Thank you, Whitfield," said Captain Smith. He half-turned to look across to his first officer. "How much time do we have, Commander Browning?"

"Several hours at best," answered Browning, studying the data on her console monitor.

"All right, everyone... let's get to work." Captain Smith swiveled his command chair slowly about. "Communications officer, I want to talk to those scientists. Science officer, life signs on the planet; and I want to know when that star is going boom. Engineering officer, finish those repairs, and get me enough energy to get us out of here. Navigation, chart me the quickest way out of here and the shortest route to Amber 3."

Captain Smith leaned on one elbow, absently rubbed at his temple. He glanced up at the viewer for the hundredth time in the last five minutes; not that there was anything to see. The planet was there, unchanged but for its slow rotation.

At least it was still there. That was something, anyway.

Saldana turned about and looked up from his station.

"Captain, the atmospheric conditions make communication with the science station impossible."

Captain Smith swiveled about, gave a dismissive nod, then turned to his first officer.

"Any sign of them?" he asked.

"Those same atmospheric disturbances make locating them difficult," said Commander Browning.

"If they're still there," said Saldana.

"Keep trying," said Captain Smith. "Both of you."

"Captain?" Underhill prompted from his engineering station.

"Lieutenant?"

"Yes... assuming they're there, and assuming we find them, we won't be able to use the transporter system."

"That is not what I want to hear, Lieutenant."

"Sorry, sir. But even if I could find a window in the disturbances, we don't have the energy. Repairs are near complete, what's left in the power rods will just get us to Amber 3. At that, shields may not hold against the nova."

Captain Smith turned to Whitfield. "Navigator, what about an alternate destination?" he asked.

"One moment." Lt. Commander Whitfield worked at her console, turned then to the captain. "Sorry, sir. The nearest station was abandoned months ago in anticipation of the impending nova. Amber 3 is the closest location."

"Very well. That'll just have to do, then."

Saldana had a finger against his earpiece, his brow furrowed as he listened.

"Captain, I'm picking up something on audio comm. Broken, fading in and out."

"I thought communication was impossible."

"Still so. Nothing I did, sir."

"Let's hear it."

Lieutenant Saldana pressed several keys. Static came over the speakers. A voice then, words and phrases and broken sentences half lost in the noise.

"Need to pick up now... four... site unstable... four to pick up... station unstable... anyone hear me?"

Captain Smith looked back to Saldana. Saldana pressed a key on his keypad, gave the captain a nod.

Captain Smith turned about again. "This is Captain Smith of Starcruiser Explorer 3," he said. "We read you."

The air filled with static, then broken "... need pick up... station unstable... anyone—"

Followed by static...

Saldana struggled to listen, to pick up something more. He looked to the captain, shook his head.

"Lost the signal, sir. I'll keep trying, but I don't know how we got anything at all."

"It was enough, Captain," said Commander Browning. "Four life signs. Lost it, but I have the coordinates."

"First good news we've heard." Captain Smith turned again to his engineer. "How do we get to 'em, Underhill?"

"There is one way, Captain. I can pilot the supply drone down to them. It'll be a tight fit, but we could take four passengers."

"The drone doesn't have life support."

"I can jury-rig something," said Underhill. "Enough to get us up from the surface."

"What *us*? You can pilot the drone from right where you're sitting."

"Too much interference, Captain. I doubt we could maintain the link; and if we lose the connection, bad things will happen."

Captain Smith thought on the idea for a long moment.

"Very well. Go," he said at last, then turned to Saldana. "Do what you can to keep a line open to the drone."

"Yes, sir," said Saldana, giving a nod.

Underhill went to the door and left the bridge as Captain Smith turned forward, looked side-glance to Commander Browning.

"Commander?" he asked, prompting.

"Nothing from the surface."

"Status of the star?"

"Monitoring," stated Browning. "The star will behave itself until it doesn't."

Whitfield gave an almost silent snicker, spoke without looking up from her work station.

"As shall we all," she said softly.

Half a dozen minutes later, Captain Smith slid from his command chair, took a slow step toward the forward viewer. The display continued to show an unchanging image of the planet.

He glanced back to Commander Browning, who said nothing as she glanced briefly up from her console.

He turned to Saldana, who was listening to his headset, one hand on the keypad of his console.

"Comes and goes, Captain," said the communication officer. He stiffened slightly then. "A moment, sir."

All on the bridge waited.

Saldana spoke into his headset.

"Got it, Underhill," he said. He frowned then. "Underhill? Underhill?"

He looked again to the captain.

"Underhill reported that he had the science station in sight, was approaching. Then... just static."

"Confirmed, Captain," said Commander Browning, her focus on her console. "Prior to losing the link, the supply drone feed was approaching station coordinates."

Anxious moments on the bridge...

Mike Saldana leaned forward, pressed a finger firmly against his earpiece, curling his brow. He spoke back to the captain.

"It's Underhill, sir." He pressed a key. The dull hiss of static came over the speakers. The voice of Lt. Underhill broke through the noise.

"Got 'em in sight," Underhill reported; several nervous moments later: "Opening access door."

There was only static, then. Saldana frowned and shook his head.

"Thank you, Lieutenant," said the captain. He stepped back to his command chair, sat and turned to Whitfield. "The second they hit the hold floor."

"Yes, sir," said Whitfield. "We're ready."

What seemed an eternity later, Commander Browning reported, "I have them, Captain. Drone is off the surface."

Captain Smith turned from Browning to Saldana. "Lieutenant?"

Saldana shook his head in answer.

Captain Smith stared at the planet displayed on the viewer. He rested his cheek on the knuckles of one hand.

They waited...

"Drone in lower orbit," said Commander Browning.

"I have Underhill," said Saldana. "Asking to come aboard."

Whitfield reached across and pressed a key.

"Cargo bay door open," she stated.

"Drone approaching," said Browning.

"Underhill reports thirty seconds," reported Saldana.

"We don't have much more than that," said Browning, focus on her console. "A minute at most, Captain; allowing time to reach minimum safe distance."

"Standing by, Captain," said Whitfield.

There were several more long, anxious moments on the bridge, all waiting, no one speaking.

"Drone ship in," Commander Browning stated calmly. "Bay door closing."

Whitfield firmly pressed a key on the keypad of her work station.

"Leaving orbit," she said.

The display switched to show the planet receding, moments later reflected the shift to light speed.

"Speed L-2," said Whitfield.

"Show me the star," said Captain Smith.

Whitfield pressed a key, the viewer displayed the system they were leaving, including the receding star. The star shrank suddenly to a pin-prick, abruptly expanded to well beyond its original size.

"There it goes," said Underhill.

"How are we looking?" Captain Smith asked his first officer.

Commander Browning was studying the data at her work station.

"Safe distance, Captain."

"Right." Captain Smith settled back in his command chair. "Now... to Amber 3."

Browning looked up from her console, looked to the viewer. The display changed again, returned to the light speed display.

The bridge lights were set to night mode; the work station consoles were glowing dully, giving the bridge faint golden shadows. Commander Browning was sitting at the captain's station. Lt. Commander Whitfield was sitting at her navigation console. Both were comfortable, relaxed, monitoring night shift operations.

The rear door slid open and Captain Smith came onto the bridge. The overhead lights came on as he worked his way to the center of the bridge.

Commander Browning slid out of the command chair and stood beside it.

"Good morning, Captain," she said.

"Commander." Captain Smith swung the chair around, sat and swiveled forward. He pulled the console to him as he queried the first officer. "Report?"

"All systems green," said Browning. "Maintaining L-2 speed. On schedule to reach Amber 3; another 30 hours."

"Excellent."

"How are our guests, Captain?"

"They slept well, I understand. Currently in the mess, enjoying breakfast."

"Very good. I think I'll join them." Browning gave a slight nod. "With your permission."

"On your way," said Captain Smith. He looked to Whitfield then. "Good morning, Whitfield."

"Sir."

The rear door opened and Saldana and Underhill came onto the bridge. Saldana moved to the communication station, Underhill to the engineering station.

Underhill spoke as he settled in.

"Lt. Commander Whitfield, transfer helm and go get some breakfast while there's still something left."

"Yeah..." Whitfield sighed, frowned. She looked from the navigation console to tactical, back to navigation. "It looks like my breakfast will have to wait."

"Lt. Commander?" asked Captain Smith.

"Another uncharted asteroid field, just coming into range."

Captain Smith looked from one to another on the bridge, mumbled aloud.

"Now what do you think the odds that we would come across a second uncharted asteroid field within a week while traveling through a fully charted sector?"

Commander Browning had moved to her own work station rather than exiting the bridge and had activated her science console.

"Incalculable, Captain."

"Right," said Captain Smith, a half-grin. To Whitfield then, "Visual, navigation?"

"Just coming up, Captain," said Whitfield. "There won't be much to see."

Dark specks began to show on the display, still very distant.

"Over, under, around?" asked Captain Smith.

"Early data indicates quite a large field," said Commander Browning.

"I wouldn't recommend much of a deviation," said Underhill. "Power rod levels are borderline as it is."

Captain Smith hesitated, studying the approaching asteroid field.

"Through the field, then," he said.

"Yes, Captain," said Whitfield.

Lt. Underhill swung about from his work station.

"Please avoid running into asteroids, Lt. Commander," he said. "We have no energy to spare for repairs."

"I'll do my best, Lieutenant."

"Slow to L-1," said Captain Smith.

"Aye, sir," said Whitfield. "L-1."

The individual asteroids showing on the forward viewer continued to grow in size as the ship approached. They were widely spaced.

"Take us to impulse," Captain Smith ordered.

"Impulse. Aye, sir," said Whitfield.

"An unidentified craft ahead," said Browning, her focus on her console. "Stationary, parked just inside the asteroid field."

"Commander?" the captain prompted.

"Just coming into sensor range."

"Have it on tactical now, Captain," said Whitfield. "Sensors not giving us much. The ship is quiet."

"Visual?"

"Just coming up."

A few moments later, the viewer shifted slightly to port, zoomed in. The ship was visible, sitting amongst a cluster of widely scattered asteroids.

"Running configuration and sensor data through the database," said Commander Browning. The data search completed. "No match, Captain."

"Well, isn't that interesting," said Captain Smith. "Anybody recognize it?"

"We have nothing comes even close, Captain," said Underhill.

"Mike," Captain swiveled about to look at Saldana. "Let's them 'em a call."

Lt. Saldana pressed several keys, sending out a preset communication. He waited, listened. He turned to the captain, shook his head.

"Sorry, Captain. No response."

Captain Smith nodded acknowledgement, turned to Browning.

"Nobody home?" he asked.

"I detect no damage," said Browning. "I do not believe it is abandoned."

"Could they be responsible?" Underhill wondered aloud.

"Lieutenant?" prompted Browning.

"For the asteroid field."

"At this point, that's a bit of a stretch."

Underhill shrugged, "Then what are they doing here?"

Captain Smith looked from Browning to Underhill. "Looking?"

Underhill gave another shrug, this one more doubtful.

Lt. Commander Whitfield turned from his station to look at the rest of the crew.

"Perhaps we should be more insistent," she said. "A harder knock on the door."

Captain Smith considered, quickly decided against it.

"They've made no threat," he said. "And while it is rude, ignoring our call is not unlawful."

Underhill was of two minds on this.

"I am suspicious regarding their presence, as I said, but if circumstances get ugly, win or lose, we can forget about reaching Amber 3."

"Understood," said Captain Smith. He gave a sharp nod to Whitfield. "Take us in, navigator. Get us through clean."

"Yes sir."

The captain settled back in the command chair, looked side-glance to his first officer.

"Put our data together, Commander," he said. "We'll turn it over once we get to Amber 3."

"Yes sir."

Commander Browning came onto the bridge. The door slid closed behind her as she started across to her work station. The forward viewer displayed an approaching planet.

Amber 3.

"Slow to impulse," said Captain Smith. He gave a short nod to Browning, kept his attention on the viewer.

"Impulse, aye," said Lt. Commander Whitfield.

On the viewer, the approach of the planet continued, now more slowly.

"Captain..." said Saldana. "I have Admiral Tanaka on comm."

"Put him on the forward viewer, Lieutenant."

Saldana pressed a key and the display on the viewer was replaced with the image of Admiral Tanaka.

"Welcome to Amber 3, Captain Smith," said the admiral.

"Thank you, Admiral. I see you got here before us."

"I understand that my journey was rather less eventful than yours."

"But not nearly so much fun, I bet."

"I imagine not," said Admiral Tanaka. "I congratulate you and your crew on the success of your mission."

"Thank you, sir; our pleasure."

"We have a transport waiting to take the scientists off your hands just as soon as you make orbit."

"They are quite eager, sir," said Captain Smith.

"No doubt," said the admiral. "And... we have been studying the reports forwarded from Commander Browning regarding the asteroid fields and the alien craft. Most interesting. We have postulated a number of possible scenarios, all of which require further data."

"I can see that, sir."

"And that is where you come in, Captain. Take a break, rest and recreate, and then you and your crew will depart on a new mission."

"Yes, sir," said Captain Smith. "I'm sure we are all looking forward to it."

"Very good." Admiral Tanaka looked briefly to someone off camera, then back to Captain Smith. "Mission data is coming to you now. Tanaka out."

The viewer went dark. The screen then reactivated with the display of the planet.

Captain Smith sat back in his command chair, looked to Commander Browning on one side, Lt. Underhill on the other. Both were wearing half smiles.

Whitfield, at the navigation station midway between the captain and the forward viewer, spoke up.

"Approaching Amber 3, Captain."

"Put us in orbit, navigation," said Captain Smith.

"Parking the ship, sir," said Whitfield, pressing keys on the keypad at his console.

Captain Smith spoke then to all on the bridge.

"You heard the admiral. Rest and recreate, everyone." He put on a sly grin. "I'll see you all back here in ten."

Underhill pressed a key, then another. "Loving the plan, sir."

The rest of the crew continued working their stations, now all with half-grins.

Fade out...

End Episode One...

Sisters in Space
Episode 1
Awakening

Introduction

This is the short story adaptation of the first episode screenplay of the seven episode webseries.

Episode One - Awakening
Claire and Amelia wake from cryo and find themselves eighty years into deep space with no idea how they got there.

The series:
The Sisters in Space collection is seven episodes adapted from seven 15 minute screenplays and follows their journey home.

Note: The short story adaptations of all seven episodes are available in an omnibus edition in paperback and ebook.

Sisters in Space – Episode 1

"Awakening"

The universe beyond the forward viewport was jet black and all but featureless. There were only a few very faint stars to indicate the cosmos wasn't totally empty.

Within the shuttle's cockpit, occasional faint beeps and tweets were the only sounds that broke the blanket silence. There was no sound of human activity, no muffled rumble of engines; nothing but the quiet existence of the shuttle's computer system going about its solitary business.

The only illumination came from tiny indicator lights on the front panel set before the view window and those in the console between the two empty seats; that and what little light managed to reach in through the narrow opening leading to the main compartment.

The main compartment was sixteen feet long, lit only by the soft glow of panels set beneath a pair of sleeper canisters that were recessed into the port wall, set behind clear plastic panels. Claire lay in the upper canister, her sister Amelia in the lower. They were dressed in beige cryo-support coveralls, monitoring and bio tubes attached to the synthetic sleeves and at the waist. They lay comfortably asleep on thick cryo-support sleeper pads.

Claire was twenty two years old. She was tall and thin, with a thin face and long, straight brown hair. Amelia was twenty years old, a few inches shorter than her sister. Her hair was wavy and several shades lighter.

Storage compartments were set into the bulkheads to either side of the sleeper canisters. Set into the opposite wall was a computer station, a small kitchen station, food storage and the shuttle's water recycler.

A narrow table was fixed to the floor in the center of the compartment, with small benches attached on either side. A door to the rear of the cabin led to a smaller compartment that held main storage and the sani-closet. Beyond this was the EVA gear room and airlock.

At the rear of the shuttle was the power room. But for the rare course adjustment to avoid one danger or another, the power room had been quiet for a very long time. Once the desired direction and velocity had been attained, there had been no need.

The shuttle traveled silently in the empty black of space, its two occupants unaware of the passage of time, deep in cryo-sleep, fed and cared for by the shuttle's bio-system, their bodies aging at the rate of three minutes with each passing month...

Several alert lights flashed in the cockpit. A series of soft beeping sounds broke the silence and a small, square panel that had lain dormant for years began to glow. Back in the main compartment, the overhead lighting turned on, set to low and providing minimal illumination. The panel below the sleeper canisters came to life and changes were made to the fluids that fed the occupants through the bio tubes.

Adjustments to cabin life support were made in preparation of the awakening passengers.

Once all was ready, each canister's clear wall panel slid aside. A few moments later, Claire opened her eyes, and then Amelia opened hers. They lay unmoving, blinking, staring uncertainly above them.

Amelia, in the lower canister, finally rolled onto her side and sat up, placing her bare feet onto the floor. She took in several long breaths, only then looked about the main compartment. She looked side-glance at a pair of feet that appeared suddenly beside her, attached to legs dangling from the upper canister.

"Is that you, Claire?" she asked dully. Her voice was raspy. She hadn't spoken in she didn't know how long.

"Yeah... me," Claire said casually, her voice just as rough. "Uh... where are we?"

"Looks like a shuttle."

"I see that. I don't remember a shuttle."

Amelia looked back behind her, into the canister. "It's the tube I went to sleep in." She looked again into the shuttle's main compartment. "This is definitely not the transport ship."

Claire slid delicately down from the upper canister, looked about the compartment as she sat beside her sister.

"This looks like a *long recon* shuttle," she said. She looked again side to side. "Small. Two person team."

"Claire? Um... how did we end up in a recon shuttle?" asked Amelia. Not that she expected an answer.

"Something must have happened to the transport. We got moved." Claire continued to study their surroundings. "The others must be in another shuttle."

"I hope so. If something did happen—"

"I'm sure they're fine, Amelia."

"There were over three hundred people on that ship."

"I'm sure they're fine," Claire repeated, this time with a bit less conviction.

They were both quiet then for a long moment, each with their own thoughts.

Uncle Marcus? Danny?

Amelia finally looked forward, in the direction of the cockpit.

"I wonder where we are," she thought aloud.

"Near Trinahr, I imagine," said Claire. "The system woke us up for a reason."

Amelia continued looking in the direction of the cockpit, but made no effort to stand up. "I expect we should find out."

"I expect so," agreed Claire. She also showed no signs of standing.

Amelia looked in the other direction then, gave a half nod and managed to get to her feet.

"Sani-closet first," she said. "I need to get cleaned up."

"Right behind you," said Claire. She watched Amelia stagger awkwardly to the rear of the compartment, and again looked forward. She stood and started toward the cockpit.

Claire slid into the pilot's chair. She took only a moment to look out the forward view window and then tried to ignore the emptiness out there.

It didn't look much like the Trinahri system they had been destined for.

She quickly scanned the various boards on the forward panel and the central console, familiarizing herself with the configuration. She reached out then and confidently touched several pads, flipped a couple of switches. Panels illuminated as the nav system came on line. An eight-inch monitor flickered to life as text and numbers displayed and scrolled.

Claire didn't like what she was reading.

She reached out to her left and ran her fingers across several other touch pads. More panels illuminated and another small monitor came to life.

The ship's autopilot confirmed what the nav system had already told her.

Claire leaned back in the pilot's seat and frowned. She looked more closely at the view outside. She was still staring out the forward view window when Amelia came into the cockpit and settled into the copilot seat. She had changed into work coveralls.

Amelia took in that same view of the outside. "Oh, that can't be good," she said.

"It's not."

"So where are we?"

"A very long way from where we should be."

Amelia was bringing up the ship's main computer on the copilot primary monitor. She stopped and looked over at her sister.

"And where is that?"

Claire sat up, leaned forward and began running her fingers across touch pads. "I don't know."

"Claire? How can you not know?"

Claire continued tapping at a panel. "We are way, way into uncharted space," she said. "I can tell how far we are from where we should be. I can give you the path we've been on. I can tell you how long we've been on that path."

"And?"

"Eighty years."

Amelia turned quickly back to the computer station, began running her fingers across the console.

"That can't be. That can't be."

"Sure it can," Claire stated matter-of-factly. "We've been traveling at twenty percent the speed of light for eighty years, fourteen days and a couple of hours; direction consistent at ninety three degrees in the wrong direction, with the rare course adjustment to avoid hazards."

Amelia fumbled with her thoughts. "Okay... okay... so what do we do?"

Claire shrugged a shoulder. "Turn around, start back."

"Another eighty years?"

"What choice do we have, Amelia?"

Amelia leaned back in her seat. She stared out at the black empty space before them. From all she could tell, they could have been sitting motionless in the dark, but Claire had just said they were travelling twenty percent the speed of light; in the wrong direction.

"Eighty out, same back. If I'm up on my math, that's one hundred sixty years," she said numbly. "Everything... everyone..."

"We don't know what happened to the others," said Claire. She was working again at one of the panels. "They could be in the same fix we are."

"Come on, Claire. That's a stretch. And that's assuming they even made it off the transport."

"And I'm going to assume that for now." She gave a slight *hmm* sound and frowned at a small screen. "This could be why we were brought out of cryo... the nav array is down."

"A blessing in disguise," sneered Amelia. She nodded sharply at the forward view. "We could still be asleep; another hundred years; a thousand years."

"Even on recycle, cryo tubes don't have supplies for a thousand years, Amelia."

Amelia frowned. "You're not making the situation any easier, Sis."

Claire ignored her, swiped a fingertip across a panel and it went dark. She looked to Amelia, then back behind them, into and beyond the main compartment.

"It's not software," she said calmly. "It's the array itself."

Amelia grew coolly serious. "Can we fix it?"

"Hope so. It's gonna take an EVA."

"Fine. I'll do it."

"No, I'll go. I have more hours, and I know navigation arrays better than you."

They stared at each other a few moments. Amelia finally swiveled her seat about.

"Fine. I'll help you suit up." She started out of the cockpit. "Let's get this over with. I want to get this bucket turned around. Every second puts us further from home."

The gear room was small compared to the main cabin. There were the two suit closets on the right, the access hatch to the airlock on the left. The open area in between was for donning the suits.

Each suit hung on a heavy hook that was set into a ceiling track. Amelia pulled one out from its closet, sliding the hook along the track, as Claire shrugged her way out of her cryo-coveralls. Underneath she wore a two piece base layer covering her from ankles to neck. She had to disconnect several fittings that held the base layer to the coveralls.

She backed into the suit, stepping into it.

Amelia supported her, holding her by the elbows.

"It's going to be clumsy, Claire," she said. "No getting around it."

"I have never liked these one size fits all suits," said Claire. "I know they say it adapts, but it never fits like my own suit."

"Well, we're a long way from our jumper, so think before every move."

"Thank you, Nana."

With all the fittings and seals in place, Amelia brought the helmet from its shelf in the closet and set it into position over Claire's head. She turned it forward and locked it down. She took a toolkit from a drawer in the closet and clipped it to Claire's suit.

"It's the standard kit."

"Got it."

Claire moved over to the airlock hatch, turned to face Amelia so that her sister could activate a panel on the chest plate. After a few moments, Amelia looked directly into Claire's helmet faceplate.

"All good, Claire. You?"

Claire read through the status lines on the internal display within her helmet. She took a moment then to evaluate how everything felt physically.

"Good to go," she said at last, giving her sister a thumbs-up. She faced the airlock's inner hatch and pressed the touchpad beside it. The door opened and she stepped through.

Amelia closed the hatch behind her sister and looked through the porthole. Claire lifted a hand and waved heavy-gloved fingers without turning. She pressed another touchpad and the outer door opened. The black of space lay before her.

She took hold of a D-clamp fastened to one end of a support line and hooked it to her suit. She took the other end and reached outside, found the recessed eyelet on the hull beside the door. Once connected, Claire allowed herself to drift out of the airlock.

Back in the main compartment, Amelia settled in front of the computer station. She pressed a fingertip to a touchpad and the monitor came to life. A few keystrokes on the smooth keyboard panel and she picked up Claire's helmet cam.

"I have your feed, Claire," she said. The tiny mic in the monitor picked up her voice and fed it to her sister's helmet. "How do you read me?"

"I read you just fine, Amelia." From the display, it looked like Claire was already maneuvering into position. "This old bus is really showing its age."

"So I see. Looks like about eighty years of micro-meteors, eh?"

Claire reached a panel cover set into the hull, the short, squat navigation array beside it. "The array looks fine, but take a look at this cover."

There was a deep indentation in the cover, and two sides were bent upward, creating an opening along the exposed seam.

"It took a heck of a hit," said Amelia.

The shifting movements of the image on Amelia's monitor indicated that Claire was studying the damage from different angles, likely looking for a way to get into the nav box.

"The latch is useless," she heard her sister say. "I'll have to pry it open."

"I don't have to tell you to watch yourself, do I?" asked Amelia. "There are some sharp edges on that cover."

"By all means, Amelia. Please do point out the dangers of the vacuum of space."

"Don't get snotty."

Claire's gloved right hand came into view on the monitor. She had a small pry tool in hand. Using it on the panel cover, it took only a few seconds to get it open. The narrow beam of light from Claire's helmet lamp exposed damaged wiring within the small compartment.

Claire sighed. "This is going to take a while."

"Take your time. I'm not going anywhere." Amelia sat back and folded her arms. "I'm not going anywhere at twenty percent the speed of light."

Claire stepped down from the cockpit and into the compartment. She was dressed now in the same work coveralls as her sister.

"Course is entered," she said. "System is still calculating burn to turn us around."

"Good, good..." Amelia nodded without looking away from the computer station's monitor. She was tapping at the keyboard panel, her expression alternating between curiosity and frustration.

Claire went to the food storage cabinet, brought out a dry ration packet and sat at the table.

"D'you find anything?" she asked. She opened the packet and began eating the bite-sized food pellets.

"Some," said Amelia. "It looks like there are media files in the log, but half are corrupted and the index is toast. If I can salvage something from the directory, I might be able to bring up one of the less damaged files; at least a piece of one."

"You'll get it," said Claire. "That's what you do."

"Yeah..." Amelia let out a distracted sigh, her focus on the monitor. "We'll see..."

Claire was about to respond to that when she hesitated, leaned forward and turned her head aside. She felt it first, and then heard it; a faint rumbling through the deck plates, through the seat and the table.

The engines were coming to life.

Amelia spoke over her shoulder, still tapping at the keyboard panel and her focus still on the monitor in front of her.

"Sounds like systems finally figured out how to get us home," she said.

"We'll be there before you know it," said Claire. She smiled and tossed another food pellet into her mouth.

There were flashes of light and shadow then from Amelia's monitor, crackling static sounds, and finally broken pieces of words.

Amelia straightened and leaned nearer the console. She brushed her fingertips across the keyboard panel. The monitor display quieted as the sounds went silent.

"Amelia?" Claire prompted, standing and coming around the table. She stood beside her sister.

"Trying. Like I said, these files are—"

"Corrupted, damaged, yeah. I got that."

The screen flickered, images flashed and disappeared; more static noise from the tiny speakers.

The frozen image of a young man flashed onto the screen, his expression as though he had been speaking and was now stuck in mid-word. He was in his early twenties, had light brown hair and a friendly face. From his look, he definitely had something worrisome on his mind.

"Danny…" said Claire, and she shifted position to be a little bit nearer her sister and the monitor. "What does our dear brother have to say?"

"Working on it," said Amelia. She was working intently at the keyboard. The image on the screen vanished and was replaced with a light blue window half-filled with rows of text and code. She brought up several smaller windows and pushed these to one side, continued entering lines and running the code.

"Well?" asked Claire.

"Bits and pieces, at best."

"I'll take whatever we can get."

"That is our only option," Amelia sighed and tapped at several more pads.

The work-windows on the screen dropped away and a new image of their brother Danny popped up. Static noise and broken bits of words crackled through the speakers and Danny's image jumped and started, eventually smoothing out.

"Good morning ladies... so..." Danny hesitated, smiled his familiar thin smile. "Surprise."

"Uh, huh..." Amelia grumbled. Claire just grinned knowingly and shook her head.

Danny's smile faded. "As you may have noticed, you're no longer in the transport. About that... a bit of an incident here, I'm afraid. The Jensauri chose now to break the truce, and they chose an attack on our transport to announce this change in policy. Our luck, eh?"

"Pretty much, yeah," mumbled Amelia.

"Since you're watching this, it means we weren't able to pick you up on the other side. Sorry about that. So, real quick here... not much time. Catch you up as best I can. Things were getting out of hand. The crew woke Marcus, what with Marcus being, *you know,* Marcus."

"Good ole' Uncle Marcus," mumbled Amelia.

The video flickered suddenly and Danny's image jumped and individual words became disconnected from one another. Half a sentence more and the display jumped again, and then again, Danny's face morphing, the audio hissing and sputtering.

"Oh, come on," Claire groaned. "It was just getting interesting."

"Like I said—"

"Yeah, yeah... bits and pieces."

Danny's image solidified but the audio continued to break apart as Danny went on.

" -- took a turn—escape chambers—released—chamber—holding our particular group of sleeper tubes—damaged—tried—not going—" There was a sudden jumble of images, and then Danny's smile froze on the screen. "More—luck—eh?"

"Wouldn't have expected anything less," said Amelia.

"Don't be a party pooper," chided Claire.

The screen display jumped and the audio crackled and hissed. Words broke and whole sentences were lost. After half a dozen frustrating seconds, the picture quieted down and the audio cleared.

"... knew from the shipping manifest that there were four survey shuttles on board. He woke me to help, and we transferred you into one of 'em." Danny glanced aside, gave a nod to someone off camera. He looked again directly at the screen. "I've set a heading for ninety degrees away from all the fun. The plan is to rendezvous with you in thirty days. Alternate meet-up location is a hundred days further out."

Danny's expression grew dark.

"You're watching this, so we missed both rendezvous points. Once again... sorry." He leaned forward, appeared to be keying something in. "So... get this bucket turned about, set a course for Trinahr, and I hope to see you in about seven months."

Seven months... The sleeper tubes had originally been programmed to wake their occupants at seven months, that being the scheduled arrival date of the transport at Trinahr. Claire and Amelia had yet to discover what had gone wrong.

Amelia grumbled, "And it looks like we missed the seven month rendezvous as well."

Danny's face unexpectedly popped out of existence. The screen went blank; the compartment was suddenly very quiet.

Amelia leaned back in her chair, continued staring at the monitor. She said nothing, was frowning.

"All right, then," Claire sighed. She looked down at Amelia. "That explains one or two things. It leaves a few holes, for sure, but gives us more than we had."

Amelia folded her arms across her chest, glanced up at her sister. "It doesn't help us any, though, does it?"

"What's to help?" Claire pushed away from Amelia and started back to the table. "We're already doing what we can; heading home. I'm just glad to know something of how we got here."

Amelia said nothing to that. She stared at the now blank screen, struggling to keep back the anguish.

Claire looked over at her sister. She let out a long breath, looked down then at her hands, fingers intertwining.

"I know, Sis..." she said softly.

Everyone was gone... everyone they ever knew...

They were alone...

Claire and Amelia worked over the next several days to make the shuttle ready for the return journey. It had travelled more than eighty years on auto, and while the ship was able to maintain and service many of the systems on its own, there were some things that were better assessed under the human eye and served by the human hand. Over that eighty years, there had been wear and tear.

While Claire was only twenty two years old, she had been qualified to pilot a shuttle for three years, performed frequent maintenance on her family's small jumper and knew it inside and out. This long-range shuttle, while different in some ways, was in most ways very similar. Claire felt absolutely comfortable preparing it for an eighty year return trip. She divided her time between the cockpit and outside running a pair of EVAs. As she had seen on her first EVA, the hull had endured hundreds of micro-meteor hits over the years. The ship's monitoring system hadn't logged any breaches, but a thorough inspection was long overdue.

Amelia meanwhile focused on the ship's computer systems, cryo-canisters and inventory. She had been working computers from the inside out since she was nine. She carried on better relationships with computer AIs than with most humans. Claire was one of the few people she got along with, and she could barely tolerate her.

Returning from her second EVA in two days, Claire stood silent as Amelia helped her out of the suit, a clumsy and awkward affair. She slipped into her coveralls as her sister slid the suit back into its locker.

"All right, Sis... what's up? You're not the bright and chipper Amelia we've all come to know and love." Claire waited expectantly as her sister secured the suit and gear in place. "That's sarcasm, by the way; something you may not be familiar with."

Amelia turned and leaned a shoulder against the wall of the locker, folded her arms and looked down at her sister, who was sitting on the small bench, slipping into her shoes.

"Ship didn't wake us because of a damaged nav system. The logs don't match. Not even close."

Claire stood up. She knew the bad part was yet to come. "Then why?"

"We were running out of time in the cryo-tubes."

Claire knew what that meant. They were a long way out in the middle of nowhere. They were deep in uncharted space and she had no idea where the nearest habitable planet might me.

"How much is left?" she asked simply.

"Maybe thirty months." Amelia pushed off the wall, stood straight. "We have all the ingredients necessary in food inventory to process more of the cryo-juice, but it takes time. And to be honest, even if I used all the rations we have, it'd only give us another forty-eight months."

"You said we had twelve years of rations. All that bubbles down to four years of cryo-juice?"

"Afraid so."

Claire sat silent for a long moment, thinking over all this new info. "Let's hold off on that for now. Twelve years rations with eyes open, and two and a half in cryo. That still leaves a lot of space between us and home."

"Hence my concern," Amelia said coolly.

Claire thought on that. She stood then, sharply.

"And well-founded concern it is, dear sister," she stated decisively. "I'm hungry. How about lunch?"

Amelia watched numbly as Claire walked over to the hatch and stepped through into the main compartment. It took her a few seconds to shake herself out of it and follow her to the main compartment.

She mumbled in disbelief. "Claire? Lunch?"

"Absolutely." Claire pulled a hot-pack out of the food locker, walked over to the warming unit and tossed it in. "And today... I deserve a hot lunch. I worked hard this morning. This old boat is cleared to go."

"But we're not," said Amelia. "We have less than a fifth of the food inventory we need, and that's including the cryo-juice. What do you suggest we do?"

Claire took the short stride to the table and sat on the edge to wait for her food to heat. She looked side-glance at her sister, gave her a gentle smile.

"Listen, Sis. Considering the course we've been on, we can't be more than a few years in uncharted space. Once our nav system can plot our position, we'll set a course for the nearest friendly habitable planet and restock." Claire winked. "No problem."

"Oh, I so wish you hadn't said that. I really don't like when you say that. It never, ever goes well when you say that."

A sharp *ding* sound came from the direction of the food warmer. Claire pushed herself from the table.

"Lunch time."

Claire and Amelia were sitting in the cockpit, each going through last minute checks of all systems. It had taken five and a half days for the ship's nav system to complete the turnaround, but they were finally on course for home.

Claire finished the final checklist of the navigation system. Amelia ran final checks on environmental systems and cryo systems.

The sisters would be going into the tubes for twelve months. It didn't make much sense to run eyes-open while in this featureless void, but they also wanted to keep some months of cryo-juice held in reserve. The compromise was to initially go in for a year, see what things looked like then.

Amelia had set the cryo-tubes to wake them at twelve months, but as a backup had also reset the low-juice alert to bring them up in the event it fell below eighteen months. Both should trigger at about the same time.

They still didn't know why they hadn't been awakened after seven months, which had been the original wake-flag.

"Checklist complete," said Claire. She set her head back against the headrest. "Nothing now but the waiting."

Amelia finished her own checklists. She swiped a fingertip across a touchpad and her monitor went black.

"Right."

"Good." Claire was looking out into the dark. Now that they were turned around, there was a new splash of stars before them. They were still very distant, but at least there were more of them. Not many more, but more. It made it all seem just a bit less ominous.

Amelia leaned back now in her copilot seat. She let out a long breath. She wasn't quite ready to go into cryo.

She looked out at that cluster of stars.

"Sure hope those look closer when we wake up."

"I just hope we wake up," said Claire playfully.

Amelia gave her a look that said *I've done all I can... what more can I do?*

Claire shook her head sadly, gave a sly grin. "Lighten up, Amelia. We'll be fine."

They sat in silence, each lost in their own thoughts, staring out into the empty black.

Amelia looked to her sister, then again forward. "You know, at some point we're going to have to actually leave the cockpit and get into the cryo tubes."

"Mmm. S'pose so."

"Yeah."

There was no rush.

~ end episode one

Sutherland House
Episode One
"Andover"

Introduction

Sutherland House is a seven hour, seven episode science
fiction miniseries following Matthew and Jennifer
Sutherland, father and daughter, in their struggle against a
secret society of immortals with extraordinary abilities and
their hidden agenda.

In Episode One:
Matthew investigates strange goings-on in a small
northwest community while he and Jennifer come to grips
with the death of Matthew's wife.
... Victor, Father of the Society, welcomes home his two
young children, recently showing sign of the Abilities.
... and nine year old Mary, living at the Academy, may be
the most powerful Member in the history of the Society.

Sutherland House Episode One "Andover"

Prolog

Sharon stood in the center of the forest clearing, bright moonlight shining down upon her. She was attractive, with long brown hair, was wearing a long, flowing white dress.

A dozen men and women stood along the perimeter of the clearing, half hidden in the shadows of the surrounding fir trees. They were dressed in contemporary street clothes, some loose fitting and fluttering in a slight breeze.

They were looking in at the forty year old woman dressed in white. They showed no emotion.

Sharon looked frightened. She turned slowly about. Those standing in the shadows continued to look into the center of the clearing, their focus on Sharon growing steadier, more determined, yet with no passion.

A woman slowly laid her head back, closed her eyes.

A second observer laid his head back and closed his eyes.

Sharon continued to spin slowly about, looking to those in the half-shadow with increasing desperation. Her long hair fluttered and flowed, caught in the twisting breeze that grew steadily stronger.

A cloud drifted in front of the silver moon and the night grew dark. Shadows pushed into the clearing from the black of the forest.

Chapter One

Matthew Sutherland drove his twenty year old Lincoln slowly through the automated gates of the Sutherland House estate, up the wandering drive through the estate grounds and toward the house itself.

Matthew looked to be about forty, but his eyes revealed that he had seen much more than four decades. He had a kind face. He wore the black armband of mourning.

The estate grounds were a mix of different styles, with a variety of shrubs, plants, walks and short garden walls, as if it had all been put together piecemeal over many years as moods changed and as the gardener discovered new things and came up with new ideas; all of which were true.

The two-storey house itself was modest and surprisingly small considering the expansive grounds and high walls that surrounded it. It was unpretentious, while at the same time stately.

Matthew came into the front foyer and tossed his keys into a dish on a small table beside the front door, walked into the living room. The house was clean and comfortable; the furniture quality without being ostentatious, a mix of styles and periods, collected over the span of many years.

He dropped down on the couch, slid back and tiredly rubbed his face. He struggled to hold onto his emotions, fighting back grief. He wasn't ready to give into it.

He sat up then, leaned forward, elbows on his knees. He looked around him at the home that he had shared with Sharon for so many years.

It all threatened to fall in on him.

He ignored the sound of the front door opening and closing. Moments later, Jennifer Sutherland came into the room from the foyer. She moved quickly to the easy chair and sat, stared at Matthew. She looked a bit irritated with her father.

She was twenty, attractive in a very natural way, being that there was nothing artificial in her looks or her manner. She was wearing a full black dress and shawl.

"You can't just walk out like that," she said. Yes. Definitely irritated, but restrained.

"Sure I can."

"No. You can't."

Matthew turned to face his daughter, his gaze lost.

"You learn that in college, did you?"

"That's rude. It was rude."

"Yeah." Matthew slid back in the couch, laid his head back and stared up at the ceiling. "I wonder if the panels are shrinking or the house is settling."

"Dad—" Jennifer tried her best to ignore the ceiling.

"Do you see that?" He asked. "There's a gap between two of the panels."

"It's been there since I was three," said Jennifer, without looking up.

Matthew brought his head forward again, straightened with a sigh. He wore a studious frown.

"School break must be about over," he said. "When do you head back?"

"I told you. I've taken leave. Jorgenson said that I can pick it up again whenever I'm ready."

"Jorgenson thinks he owes us something."

"He does owe us something."

Matthew rubbed his face again, sighed.

"You shouldn't have done that, Jen. You don't want to fall behind."

"Don't worry about that, Dad. I'll be fine."

"This is your senior year."

"I'm fine."

Matthew stared a Jennifer for a long moment, then turned away. He stared absently up at the ceiling, at the gap between two of the panels.

"What a crappy day."

Jennifer leaned forward, rested her elbows on her knees. She looked carefully at her father. She appeared about to cry, pushed it back.

"I love you, Dad."

The room fell silent; the house was suddenly very empty.

"I guess it's you and me now, Jen," said Matthew.

Jennifer stood then and went over to her father. She sat beside him. They held onto each other.

"We'll be all right," she said, consoling.

"I know," he managed to say. "I know."

Matthew took the narrow stairs down to the basement. To one side were free-standing shelves filled with neatly labeled home-canned jars of fruits and vegetables. The other side of the basement contained a small workshop. There was a workbench with a set of shelves beside it.

Matthew reached into the set of shelves and released a hidden latch. There was a metallic click. The shelves swung open, gliding easily, revealing a shaft with a ladder leading down.

He stepped into the shaft, onto the ladder, started down.

He climbed off the ladder and into "the Apartment". The lights came on automatically as he walked into the room.

The Apartment was comfortable contemporary, high-tech mixed with the every day. There was an opening in the wall behind him with the shaft leading up to the main house. On either side of the shaft opening were built-in shelves filled with books. A door along the wall to Matthew's right led to the armory, another to the bathroom. There was a counter beyond, behind which was a small kitchen.

Set into the wall on Matthew's left was a large viewing screen, beside that a bank of computer monitors, five across and four rows high.

A door in the far wall opened to a long hallway leading to an underground garage. To the left of the door were racks of computer network, server and communications equipment. Beside these was a computer station with desk and chair.

There was a living area in the center of "The Apartment", with couch and chair, a round kitchen table and chairs.

Matthew took off his jacket and tossed it onto the couch, revealing that he was wearing a shoulder holster and weapon. He walked across the room to the armory closet as he slipped out of the holster. A mix of sophisticated weaponry and standard weapons were mounted on one wall of the closet. He hung up his holster, unloaded and set the pistol into its slot.

He came out of the armory and went into the small bathroom. He spoke as he washed his hands and face.

"Computer," he said, impassively.

"Yes, Matthew?" came from hidden speakers. The computer voice sounded almost human, but with a lack of true emotion behind the words and an almost too perfect quality to the syntax and pronunciation.

Computer did strive, however, to inject familiarity into the conversations that it held with Matthew and Jennifer, previously with Sharon.

Matthew quickly dried his hands and returned to the main room, started into the kitchen.

"Anything more on Sharon's death since your last report?" he asked.

"All three regional newspapers carried the obituary," stated Computer. "No additional articles. No newspapers outside the local area contain any reference. There has been no mention of Sharon Sutherland in any monitored television broadcast, radio broadcast or Internet news feeds."

Matthew took a can of iced tea out of the refrigerator and returned to the main area.

"Items of interest," he requested flatly.

"Forty-eight items identified for your review."

Matthew frowned, moved slowly to the couch. He sat down, opened the can of iced tea.

"Any that could possibly relate to Sharon's death?"

"No possible connections identified."

"Are any of the items Red Priority?"

"I have identified six items identified as Red Priority."

Matthew hesitated, absently rubbed at his temple.

"Not now." He stretched out on the couch, set the can on the floor. "Dim lights."

The lights dimmed, leaving only a faint glow in the room. Tiny red indicator lights inset into the computer equipment all about the room occasionally flickered.

Matthew rolled onto his side and immediately fell asleep.

Jennifer stood over her father, asleep on the couch. She placed a hand on his shoulder. He woke, sat up.

"Good morning," she said.

"'morning…" he looked curiously at the blanket that had been covering him, set it aside. "Morning?"

Jennifer turned away and started toward the kitchen. She obviously knew her way around the Apartment.

"I'll bet you're hungry," she said.

"A bit."

Jennifer began rummaging about cabinets and the refrigerator.

"I'll fix us something while you get cleaned up."

Matthew mumbled unintelligibly on his way to the bathroom.

Jennifer began cutting up fruit. She heard the shower running.

"Computer?" she asked.

"Hello, Jennifer," came the voice of Computer. "I am pleased to hear your voice. I have missed you."

"Thank you, Computer. I've missed you, too,"

"How is your education coming?"

"I have no doubt that you know exactly how I am doing."

"Grades are not fully representative of how someone is doing, Jennifer."

Jennifer smiled, put the plate of fruit on the counter.

"I'm doing fine," she said.

"I am pleased to hear that," said Computer.

"Anything new on Mom's murder?"

"No, Jennifer. I am sorry."

"Thank you."

There was a long pause then. The only sounds came from the running computer equipment and the low thrum of the running shower.

"I liked your mother very much," said Computer.

"Me too, Computer," said Jennifer.

Chapter Two

Jennifer was standing in the kitchen, opposite Matthew sitting at the counter. They were eating a breakfast of fruit and toast, with juice. Matthew was dressed comfortably, refreshed after his shower.

"Nothing new on Mom," said Jennifer.

Matthew only nodded, continued eating.

"Dad, I've been thinking." Jennifer started then, cautiously. "I think I should come into the business right away."

Matthew put down his fork, a chunk of cantaloupe still speared, and picked up his glass of juice.

"You need to finish school," he said. He took a drink.

"I can help you."

"No." Another swallow of juice.

"I was going to join you and Mom soon enough anyway."

"Things have changed."

"They certainly have," she said.

Matthew stared down at his glass, fought a number of emotions, all of which threatened to show themselves on his stone face.

"Your coming into the family business... it wasn't supposed to—"

"I understand that, Dad. I do." Jennifer started to reach a hand across the counter, pulled it back. "You can't do this alone."

"Jen..." Matthew let the thought fade.

One of the red indicator lights beneath the monitor set into the wall next to the counter began to flash. A small label under the light read 'Main Gate'.

A moment later the monitor activated. It showed a young man, about twenty years old, standing near the communication box at the gate. He had the look and manner of the kid next door.

"It's Sam," groaned Jennifer.

"I doubt he's here to see me," said Matthew.

"Computer... activate," said Jennifer, her tone surrendering. "Hello, Sam."

"Jennifer," said Sam, leaning nearer the communication box. His voice sounded tinny coming through the speaker. "I wanted to make sure you were all right."

"I'm fine, Sam."

"When your dad left like that... and then you—"

"We're okay, Sam. I'm sorry we ran out."

"No!" Sam said quickly. "That's all right. Everyone understood."

There was a long pause. Sam looked about, looked to the camera.

"Are you going to let me in?" he asked then.

Jennifer looked irritably over at Matthew, who had miraculously regained his appetite and was busily finishing up the fruit.

"Sure," she sighed. "Computer, monitor off."

The monitor went blank. Jennifer pushed away from the counter and started out of the kitchen.

"Main gate open," she said, starting toward the ladder.

"Thanks for breakfast," said Matthew, his focus across the counter, as he picked up his juice glass. "You kids have fun."

"And another thing, Dad," she said, climbing onto the ladder. "A ladder? A lousy ladder?"

She disappeared into the shaft. The sound of her voice became muffled, only her legs visible.

"All the money spent putting this place together, and you couldn't spring for an elevator?"

Matthew's smile came and faded. He pushed away from the counter, walked around and into the kitchen. He put the breakfast dishes into the dishwasher, cleaned the counter. He drifted into the center of main room and stood behind the couch. He looked at the rows of inactive monitors, then at the large wall display, currently dark.

"Computer," he said.

"Yes, Matthew?"

Matthew stared dully at the wall.

"Nothing," he said.

Matthew felt very, very alone.

§

The Academy grounds were eerily empty of people, despite it being mid-afternoon, the day sunny and warm. There were several old, stately buildings of brick and ivy. The grounds themselves were green lawns and wide, winding walkways. Several hundred feet from the main building stood a large, ancient oak tree, hovering over a wide walkway running from the small parking lot to the main administration building.

A nine year old girl was standing in the window of her room, looking out at the grounds and the large oak tree.

Mary's face was reflected in the glass. The quarters behind her were small; a single narrow bed, a desk and chair; there was a door to the closet, a larger door leading out to the hall.

Mary continued to look contemplatively outside. There was a sadness about her.

She lifted her gaze slightly. Despite the fact that there could be no breeze, her hair began to flutter.

She closed her eyes.

Her hair brushed back from her face against a breeze that did not exist.

The lights of the Apartment had gone dim. Matthew was standing behind the couch, looking across the room at the far wall. He slowly turned his head, lifted his gaze and looked up and to one side.

There was something...

He sensed... something.

Chapter Three

Jennifer stepped off the ladder and into the Apartment.

The lights were on. Several of the monitors in the far wall were on, displaying nebulous scenes from security cameras located in unremarkable office buildings.

"Computer, where's Dad?" she asked.

"Matthew is in the garage, Jennifer."

Jennifer walked across the room and opened the door in the opposite wall. She entered a long, narrow hallway, lit by several ceiling light panels evenly spaced along the hall.

She opened the door at the far end of the hall and walked into the underground garage.

It looked much like an auto service center. Along the left side were six stalls containing an assortment of vehicles: a 64 Comet, an old Bronco, a small converted school bus, a late model BMW, a 97 Ford pickup, a pair of dirt bikes, and a Harley-Davidson Sportser.

On the right was a line of service bays; a chest-high counter spanned the length of the wall.

At the far end, an opening to a tunnel that curved away and out of sight.

Jennifer moved along the line of vehicles until she found Matthew under the hood of the immaculate 1964 Mercury Comet.

"Dad?"

Matthew answered from under the hood: "Yeah."

"Dad, what are you doing?" She sounded disheartened.

"I'm walking the dog."

"Dad..."

"Jennifer, I'm working on the car." He continued to speak from under the hood. "The car needs work—I'm working on it."

Jennifer watched Matthew work for several seconds before trying again.

"Listen, I'm not trying to push you, but it's been almost two weeks. I'm not asking that you to take on anything major, but at least let Computer run you through the Red Priorities."

"Computer will let me know if there's anything vital."

"Isn't that what 'Red Priority' means?"

Matthew remained under the hood.

"Not this week, it doesn't."

Jennifer folded her arms and looked sympathetically at her father, half his body under the hood. When she spoke again, there was a quiet desperation in her voice.

"I'm sorry, but I'm not going to let you just walk away. The Business is too important. Like it or not, you have a responsibility that you can't ignore."

Matthew finally came out from under the hood. He picked up a red rag and began cleaning the open-end wrench that he brought out with him.

"I'm not walking away from anything. I know how important the Business is. I did start it, after all. The work isn't stopping just because I spend a few days taking care of some things I've been neglecting.

"Is that what you're doing?" she asked, flatly.

Matthew looked coolly at his daughter, spoke now in a lecturing tone.

"Computer continues its daily scan of every newspaper to hit a computer system or news item to hit the wires. It continues its twenty-four hour a day monitoring of three hundred forty-three television stations and six hundred twelve radio stations."

"I know that," Jennifer stated precisely.

Matthew put down the wrench and picked up another, continued cleaning his tools.

"As we speak," he went on, "it is monitoring security systems of key locations throughout the United States and select International locations. It is monitoring Internet sites and Internet communications. It is monitoring the telecommunications activity of one thousand two hundred and four key people throughout the world. It is also tracking stock markets, financial markets, monetary values and agricultural markets, as well as numerous financial institutions."

He paused, put on a sardonic smile.

"And it is managing our portfolio. I do believe we are quite well off."

"I lack for very little," Jennifer said in a low grumble.

Matthew put down the second wrench, began methodically cleaning sockets.

"Computer continually bounces all that data around; storing, rearranging, collating, filing, processing, recalculating... and when two or more items come together just right, Computer puts in on the list. When I'm ready, Computer shows me that list. Now... when it's important enough, Computer hits me over the head with it, whether I'm ready or not."

"You have Red Priority items," said Jennifer, determined. "That makes them important."

"They'll keep." Matthew began putting his clean tools into the tall, red tool chest beside him. He indicated the nearby Bronco. "Right now, I need to realign the Bronco."

"I'll do it."

"I like doing it."

"So do I," said Jennifer.

Jennifer pulled the Bronco into one of the service bays. She climbed out of the vehicle and began hooking up the alignment equipment to the front, left tire.

She stood when she heard the sound of the Comet starting, watched as it backed out of the stall and head for the tunnel.

The tunnel was several hundred feet long, wide enough and tall enough for a small bus and not much more. Security cameras were mounted at several locations along the way. A sensor along the route activated and a red light turned off, the green light turned on. The access door opened.

The Comet passed through, started out onto an isolated dirt road, grassy foothills and scattered oak trees and brush. The metal access door glided smoothly and quietly closed behind it.

Back in the garage, Jennifer knelt and began making adjustments to the alignment apparatus.

"Computer, where is Dad going?" she asked.

"Indications suggest Rydel Ridge." Computer directed his voice to the nearest speaker. "Would you like me to ask him?"

Jennifer continued preparing the alignment equipment.

"No," she grumbled.

Rydel Ridge was a lookout point with a small picnic area and parking lot. It was surrounded on several sides by a grove of trees. Downslope below the ridge was a meadow frequented by deer.

Matthew was sitting on the hood of the parked Comet. His was the only car. He was alone.

The silence was interrupted by the sound of another vehicle approaching. A small car came into the lot and pulled up near Matthew.

A teenager climbed out.

"Excuse me," he said. "Did you order the pizza?"

Matthew slid off the hood.

"You're new," he said warily.

"Sir?"

"Never mind."

The delivery person walked around to the passenger side of his car and pulled a pizza box out of a red warmer sleeve. He also came up with a small cardboard box.

"Medium combination, potato salad, and a liter of root beer."

"Did you remember the ice and a cup?" asked Matthew.

"Right here, sir," indicating the cardboard box. "Also, napkins and a fork."

Matthew took the pizza box and set it on the hood. The delivery person set the cardboard box down beside it and pulled a receipt out of his pocket.

"Your receipt," handing it to Matthew.

Matthew dropped it into the box, then handed the teenager a ten dollar bill.

"Everything looks to be here," he said.

"Aim to please." The teenager shoved the bill into his pocket and hurried back to his car.

Matthew watched him until the car was out of sight, then climbed back onto the hood. He slid the pizza box to one side of him, the cardboard box to the other.

He brought out the container of potato salad, dug around for the fork. He sat back then and continued to enjoy the day.

Finished with the alignment, Jennifer returned to the Apartment and cleaned up, then sat at the computer station. She brought up the vehicle maintenance log, began entering information on the work she'd done.

"Computer?" she prompted as she worked.

"Yes, Jennifer?"

"Sorry to bother you again..."

"Jennifer, you know very well that I am capable of carrying on conversations and responding to your requests and queries while simultaneously performing my other duties."

"Yeah, yeah, yeah... is Dad still at the Ridge?"

"The sensor indicates that Matthew is not in the vehicle. Once he left the immediate area surrounding Sutherland House, visual surveillance was discontinued. Monitoring indicates, however, that a delivery of pizza, potato salad and Mug root beer was made to Robert Matthews at the Rydel Ridge picnic grounds approximately twenty-three minutes ago. Robert Matthews is one of Matthew's current aliases."

Jennifer continued typing while half-listening to Computer.

"Sounds like his diet," she said.

"Would you like me to attempt to establish visual surveillance of the Rydel Ridge area?"

"No." Jennifer leaned back in her chair. "Let him know that I'm watching him."

There was a long pause as Computer relayed her message through the communications system in the Comet, then waited for a reply.

"Your father conveys his deep appreciation for your concern regarding his wellbeing."

Jennifer snickered at this, gave the maintenance log a final onceover before closing it, then stood and pulled a wireless keyboard from a shelf. She activated it as she started toward the couch.

"Transfer to main display, please," she said. "Bring up my game project."

The main wall display lit up as she reached the couch, her application development screen filling the display. She plopped her body down and set the keyboard in her lap.

"I am pleased to see you working on your game again, Jennifer."

Jennifer looked at one and then another of the windows on the display, each filled with C code. She moved one to the side, then another, expanded a third.

"Not much chance at school," she said. "And here... well, lately... you know."

Chapter Four

Dianna Broderick entered the front foyer of the fine home. She looked to be in her forties. She was trim and well-maintained, wore a well-tailored dress, and had the look and air of a woman born to the life of refinement.

Two young children stood in the foyer beside their nanny. Robby was six, Thomas five.

Dianna bent down and gave each child a gentle hug. She straightened then, gave a nod to the nanny.

"Mrs. Evans," she stated flatly.

"Good morning, Mrs. Broderick," said Mrs. Evans.

"Mr. Broderick is waiting for them in his office."

"Yes, ma'am. I'll take them up."

Victor Broderick stood in front of his desk, his eye on the door. He was a tall, distinguished gentleman, looked to be in his fifties, with all the air of a high-placed, well-bred individual, fully accustomed to being in control and in charge.

Just now he was nervous.

The door opened and Mrs. Evans ushered in the two young children. They stood quietly before Victor.

"And whom do we have here, Mrs. Evans?" he asked.

Mrs. Evans placed a hand on one shoulder of each child.

"Robby, Thomas… say hello to your father."

Robby spoke in a calm, polite tone. "Hello, Father."

Thomas looked up at Victor but said nothing.

"Hello, boys," said Victor. "I've missed you."

There was an awkward silence. Victor finally clasped his hands behind his back and looked calmly down at his children. With only the slightest indication from him, Mrs. Evans moved into action.

"Off we go now, boys," she said. "You'll see your father at dinner."

Victor watched the nanny shuffle them through the door and out of sight. He stared at the open doorway.

There was absolute silence.

With a twitch of two fingers of his left hand, the door closed with a soft thump.

He stood alone in the quiet room.

Matthew was alone in the Apartment. The lights were dim.

He walked to the couch but remained standing.

"Computer. Activate main screen."

The wall screen lit up, though there was no data. Matthew didn't move. He stared at the wall, now faintly aglow.

"Computer..." Matthew's word drifted away into silence.

Computer waited.

"Computer..." said Matthew. Again he hesitated. Finally then, "What say we review the Red Priorities?"

"Yes, Matthew."

The picture of a young woman appeared on the display.

"The first item is the murder of Marli Reynolds."

A series of police crime scene photographs began to display, one photograph at a time.

Matthew sat down as Computer continued to review.

"Age seventeen, her body found along the bank of the Sacramento River. She was murdered elsewhere, her unclothed body dumped at the discovery site."

"Reynolds?" asked Matthew. "Doesn't ring any bells."

"Miss Reynolds' cousin, Karen Lawrence, with whom she had a close relationship, is married to Mark Gryphen."

"Son of Phillip Gryphen," stated Matthew.

"That is correct."

The photo displayed on the wall was of Marli Reynolds' naked, bruised and broken body twisted among smooth, rounded river rocks.

Matthew calmly studied the photograph.

"How was she murdered?"

A new photo displayed on the screen, this one showing Marli Reynolds on an autopsy table.

"Reports state that there was minimal bruising on the neck, yet severe internal damage."

A series of newspaper articles displayed.

"That fact was not made public," Computer continued. "There was mention of the murder on each of the local television news programs immediately following the discovery of the body, with an accompanying statement that cause of death was yet to be determined. Similar news stories were broadcast on the local radio stations."

"Just another murdered kid," said Matthew.

"Three regional newspapers carried the story, two of which had follow-ups several days later. Once again, however, the circumstances of the death were never revealed."

"The current status of the case?"

Marli Reynolds' high school picture displayed.

"Open," said Computer. "No activity. One detective assigned, and she is also working on several other cases."

Matthew stood, walked toward the picture of Marli.

"Give me the autopsy report," he said.

The first page of the report displayed. It wasn't the image of a hardcopy, but rather a computer template populated with data. Matthew read, his face shimmering against the glow of the display.

"The authorities didn't get all this, did they?"

"No."

The display changed, showed a printed hardcopy of the report. A few moments later, the hardcopy and the computer template displayed side by side.

Matthew took a moment to compare them.

"If the M.E. was trying to hide something, why bother entering one set of data into the computer and then send out a hardcopy with a different set of data?" He turned from the display. "Have you checked to see if the data on file has changed since you first acquired this information?"

"The data on file has not changed," said Computer. "It is not consistent with the data received by the authorities."

"The difference between the two?"

"The hardcopy report contains no mention of the severity and peculiarities of the neck injuries. While the computer data identifies these injuries as the cause of death, the hardcopy report lists the cause of death simply as strangulation."

Matthew returned to the couch and sat down.

"I didn't see possible method," he said.

"None was specified."

"So, we have Marli Reynolds. Tenuous connection to one of the Families. Said young lady is found murdered. Her body is obviously meant to be discovered, and in front page, albeit brief, fashion. Cause of death is unusual, and said cause is hidden from not only the public but also from the authorities."

He quickly corrected himself...

"Although the true report may have reached the authorities and was subsequently switched."

"A plausible supposition," said Computer. "Given the current facts."

"A rather violent way to get rid of a problem, isn't it? The Gryphens are nothing if not subtle."

"They may have been hoping a connection would be made to several similar murders committed in previous weeks," said Computer. "A possible connection was investigated and ruled out."

"Or perhaps someone in the family did a little independent activity," said Matthew.

"Members of the Gryphen Family are not known for independent activity."

"Oh, you can bet Phillip Gryphen is seriously peeved." Matthew grew thoughtful, then came to a decision. "Continue this one on your own, Computer. You're probably right about a Society tie-in, and I would certainly like to take a crack at the Gryphens, but—"

"I will keep you informed," stated Computer.

"Next item."

The display now showed a photograph of a middle-aged man. The picture could easily be a driver's license photograph.

"Cult leader John Cutler," said Computer. "Government sources have identified his true name as Jon Willeby."

The display changed, showing John Cutler speaking before a crowd.

Computer continued.

"There have been numerous reports of Cutler performing miracles."

"That certainly wouldn't draw your attention, and most definitely not flag it as a Red Priority. I therefore assume there is a lot more going on here than simply a miracle worker at work."

"Of course," said Computer.

"Oh... I sense annoyance."

"On the contrary. I am nothing if not content... and patient."

"Okay..." Matthew said slowly. "Go on."

The reflection from the display showed on Matthew. The pale shadows on his face shifted as the display changed.

Mary's quarters, the Academy; the rays of the setting sun were streaking in through the window, brushing across her face as she sat in her chair.

There was a sense of timeless calm in the room.

That calmness shown on Mary's face.

The Academy Headmaster eased into the chair behind his desk. He had a kind look about him. In his fifties, he had begun to gray about the edges and had a bit of late middle-aged spread.

The same sunset colors shone through the small window of his office.

There was a light on in the outer office that shone through the frosted glass pane set into the only door. The word "Headmaster" was stenciled on the glass, reverse image as seen from this side of the door,

As the Headmaster sat, the glow of the computer monitor before him reflected on his face. He stared at the words that he had written.

He spoke then, and his words appeared on the screen.

"Mary is progressing faster than we anticipated; faster than we dared hope. I sometimes sense that she is actually holding back so that we can keep up with her. As you will see in this week's enclosed report, she continues to show tremendous advancement in all six Abilities. As you well know, such is almost unprecedented. While ten percent of Society members do in fact possess talent in all six Abilities, very few of that ten percent have evidenced such latent power in all of them—and I have never witnessed such potential."

There was a long, ominous pause.

"Sir, I believe..." he paused again, began again. "I believe that Mary is much greater than we originally assessed."

The Headmaster grew silent, stared uneasily at the words on the screen.

Chapter Five

Matthew walked around the couch with a can of iced tea in hand. He climbed onto the couch and sat on the back, always with an eye to the main display on the wall. Spreadsheet text was displayed in a data window on the display; data on the third Red Priority item that Computer had presented.

Or was it the fourth...

Matthew opened the can, took a long drink.

"All right, let's go on to the next one," he said. "This one bores me."

The displayed cleared.

"I will continue monitoring this item and keep you apprised of any developments," said Computer.

"You do that," said Matthew. "Next."

A photocopy of a newspaper article appeared on the display wall.

"The community of Andover, located in Washington State."

Matthew slid down on the couch, took another swallow.

"Make it interesting."

"Andover has a population of just over two thousand," said Computer. "It has its own hospital, doctor, dentist, water district, K-8 school, retirement center, police force, volunteer fire and emergency station, as well as a handful of stores and restaurants. There is also a lumber mill, a dairy, and several farms."

"Nice setup," said Matthew. "Nothing sinister, though. There must be hundreds of little empires just like it."

"Many small communities manage to establish some level of self-sufficiency. Few, however, have realized the level of independence as has Andover."

Photographs displayed in sequence, showing a small town nestled in the woods. These were followed by several official documents that looked to be permits, ownership certificates and business licenses.

"Can you tell me what drew you to some three-inch fluff story that a bored cub reporter dug up at county records?"

asked Matthew. "And just how it has anything to do with us?"

"It is true that the item first came to my attention as a result of a small story in a weekly newspaper. It described the turnaround and subsequent success of the town of Andover. Further investigation subsequently revealed this to be in fact a Red Priority item."

Jennifer was behind the wheel, driving the small bus down a rural, county road. There were no storefronts or homes; only an occasional lone vehicle that passed in the opposite direction.

Computer's voice disrupted the sense of solitude, coming from a speaker set in the dash.

"Jennifer?"

"Yes, Computer?"

"Your father would like to speak with you."

"Patch him through," said Jennifer.

"Jennifer." Matthew's voice sounded distant, hollow.

"Yes, Dad."

"I hear you're doing a bit of tinkering. How's the bus?"

"The rebuild on the carb did the trick," she answered.

"It just needed your magic touch," said Matthew. "Will you be coming back soon?"

"I'm about ten minutes out. Is there a problem?"

"Not at all. I think we may have an assignment."

"We?"

"If you're interested."

"I'm on my way."

Matthew and Jennifer were sitting at the table, papers scattered about on the tabletop, along with a can of iced tea and a half-full glass of water. The wall display behind them showed one of the exterior shots of the town of Andover.

"Andover was just another mill town," said Matthew. "It had a grocery store, a gas station, VFW hall, tavern, and a few hundred houses all about half a century old. But a couple of things it had going for it that most other towns of a couple of thousand people didn't have was a hospital sitting on one hill, and a school on another."

Jennifer picked up and studied a document.

"I'm guessing things started to change about... four years ago."

"About the time the mill was bought up." Matthew tapped at the document in Jennifer's hands. "It had been privately owned, but was closely allied with one of the big lumber companies. The purchase price wasn't publicly disclosed, but it was rumored, and Computer has verified, that the new owners considerably overpaid for the mill."

"Why?"

"Don't know." Matthew picked up his iced tea, took a swallow, set it back on the table. "Once they had it, they began making changes. They severed all the original ties, and lost the mill's customer base. The employees really started sweating it, especially when the mill shut down for retooling. But the new owners kept the workers on, using them to help with the renovation. They even gave raises when they reopened a few months later. The mill began bringing in its raw materials from outside the traditional markets, and began acquiring customers from the Midwest.

"So the new owners brought their suppliers and their customers with them."

"Seems that way."

"Society?"

"The connection isn't as strong as it might be, but Computer leans to yes."

"Why?"

"Not there yet," sighed Matthew. "But here are some interesting tidbits. At about the same time the mill was changing hands, the town council began changing hands as well. An overworked group of six community leaders paid a token salary of one dollar a month each. Nonetheless, they wielded what power there was in town. The town mayor had held leadership of the council for twenty-two years and showed no signs of ever letting go. Then, in a sudden and surprising turn of events, he and two others of the council were voted out, replaced by relative newcomers."

"And these have been identified as Society."

"Not yet, but..." Matthew spoke then over his shoulder. "Computer, time for some pictures."

"Please be more specific, Matthew."

"Let's start with the Addisons and go on from there."

A moment later the display showed a photograph of Robert Addison. The photograph moved to one side, allowing room for Linda Addison. Both looked to be in their thirties.

"Robert and Linda Addison," Computer stated.

Matthew turned to Jennifer.

"The Addisons showed up in Andover about four years ago."

"The same time as—"

"Right," said Matthew. "Robert is a freelance computer expert, occasionally consults to big business, writes tech books. Linda is a teacher, and it is this that is supposed to have brought them to Andover. There was an opening at the school."

The display changed. A photograph of an older man appeared. This photograph moved to one side, allowed room for a photograph of a woman. Both appeared to be in their sixties.

"Daniel and Emma Chandler," said Computer.

"Both retired," said Matthew. "Showed up in Andover a week after the Addisons. Daniel Chandler was a city planner, and Emma had been an administrator for a retirement community.

"Sounds ominous," said Jennifer, a mocking tone.

"It's all very innocent. A rundown mill gets a lift, a town council gets some new blood, a few new folks move in, breathe life into a stagnant community." Matthew stared at his can of iced tea. He took another drink. "But there's more going on. The revitalization of Andover has been carefully orchestrated. The people coming into town aren't random. Their talents mesh just a little too perfectly with the needs of the town, always at just the right time."

"Interesting," said Jennifer. "And?"

"And... Remember that I said there's been a slow influx of new people over the years. Most small towns get the occasional newcomer, but Computer has identified a point in time, beginning about six years ago, when Andover began a steady, consistent migration of new people."

"Preparing the way?"

"Which means the work actually began six years ago, not four. But the more interesting part of this is that the actual population has remained about the same."

"Oh. Very sci-fi," said Jennifer. "The town's being replaced."

"Uh-huh."

"You brought up the Addisons and the Chandlers. They've been identified as Society?"

"Still working on it," said Matthew. "I brought them up in particular because they seem to be at the center of a lot of what is going on there; as mundane and ordinary as that activity appears to be. Computer has their new names and backgrounds, their photographs, and the dates they showed up. The names and backgrounds are forged, the faces may or may not have been altered, but there are paper trails starting the day they entered Andover. Computer is working on that."

Computer displayed another picture on the wall. It was of a middle-aged man, nondescript, with no supporting text.

"Walter Carlson," said Computer.

Matthew glanced up at the image.

"Carlson, the mayor of Andover," he said. He hesitated then, looked away.

"Dad?" asked Jennifer.

Matthew's thoughts were taking him down an uncomfortable path. He looked down at his iced tea, pushed the can aside with two fingers.

"What is Victor up to?" he asked, as much to himself as to Jennifer.

Victor stood at the second floor window of his home office. Looking through the glass, he watched the two children, Robby and Thomas, in the playground that took up the left side of the backyard. The yard contained a Jungle Jim, swing set, clubhouse, and assorted bar and climbing apparatus.

The children were playing on the bars as Mrs. Evans sat on a nearby bench reading a book.

Thomas suddenly fell from the bars. Mrs. Evans was up in an instant, but almost immediately sensed that the child was unhurt. She calmly sat back down and returned to her reading.

Robby hurried to help his little brother.

Victor turned from the window. He noted a message box flashing on his computer monitor. He returned to his desk, pushed aside the chair and stood before the monitor. He clicked a key on his keyboard. The message box disappeared. He looked over at the speaker phone.

He activated the phone with a thought. A light began blinking and the sound of the dial tone could be heard.

"Get me Carlson," said Victor.

The sound of the dial tone was replaced with the sound of numeric tones as the phone dialed.

There were two rings and the phone picked up.

"Yes?" came over the phone.

"Mayor Carlson," Victor said, harshly. "What the hell is going on in Andover?"

"Mr. Broderick—" Carlson started.

"There continue to be inquiries into our activities," said Victor. "I need your assurance that all is being done that can be done to guarantee our anonymity in Andover."

"All is being done that can be done, sir."

Victor walked back to the window, looked out at his children. He spoke over his shoulder in the general direction of the phone.

"The Andover community presents the greatest threat of exposure that we have ever faced. The peril is not only of our detection, but of our destruction."

"From Andover will come our greatest power," said Carlson through the phone's speakers.

"It is not power that we seek from Andover. It is the survival of the Society." Victor turned from the window and returned to his desk. "I've been looking over the latest reports. The conclusions from the most recent research are not as encouraging as I would hope."

"The arrival and integration of several families of... *minimal*... Abilities. This distorted the results of some of our experiments. You may also have noted the misguided directions of several Members in regards to the research. I have talked with them."

Victor responded with forced patience: "I encourage exploration, Mayor. And understand this—every member of the Society holds equal value. No one's Abilities diminish our strength—we are made stronger."

"Yes, sir," the mayor said hesitantly.

"Your reports will reflect factual data, not pretentious snobbery," Victor said sharply. "Phone off."

The light on the phone went off. Victor walked around his desk. He held out a hand and his coat came floating to him from across the room in a rush. He grasped it.

The door opened as he approached it.

Walking the second floor mezzanine, he "spoke" in *thought talk* to his wife, his words reaching out to her mind-to-mind.

"Dianna, I am more than ready for lunch. How about you?"

His wife's voice came to his mind as he reached the stairs.

"I'll be ready before you get downstairs," she said.

"On my way."

Chapter Six

Jennifer was sitting on the couch in the Apartment, reviewing the data on Victor Broderick with Computer. She was not unfamiliar with the information, but had not been around it much over the last few years.

There was a photograph of Victor on the display wall. Beside the photograph was a data window filled with text describing his Family.

Computer was providing details.

"Victor Broderick. Born 1878, Boston Massachusetts. Current residence, Boulder Colorado. He is the third Father of the Society, taking the position twenty-eight years ago upon the death of Albert Broderick, who was in turn the protégé of Jonas Westerman, the First Father and one of the three brothers who founded the Society three hundred and sixteen years ago."

The photograph on the display wall changed to one of Dianna Broderick.

"Dianna Broderick is Victor Broderick's second wife," Computer continued. "They have been married twelve years. Victor has three grown children from his first marriage and two young children from this, his second. All are Society, with his two youngest children only recently showing signs and subsequently gaining membership."

The display changed again, now showed two photographs: one of Robby and one of Thomas.

"There had been some concern," said Computer, "as both Robby and Thomas were late in showing sign."

"What are their Abilities?" asked Jennifer.

"I have yet to access information regarding the nature of their Abilities."

"Victor has four," recalled Jennifer. "How many does Dianna have?"

"Dianna Broderick has two—thought talk and telekinesis, both at high levels."

Jennifer nodded slowly, her mind drifting. Possessing two of the six Abilities was fairly common among Society members. Victor having four was rare; possessing four at high levels was very rare.

"Victor's grown children... if I remember right, they're not that much older than I am."

Three photographs appeared on the display, one at a time, each making way for the next until they were all showing side by side.

"Vincent, Carl and Anna," said Computer. "All are in their thirties."

"Which means Victor waited quite a while before having children."

The displayed changed again, this time to a candid photograph of Victor and an unidentified woman walking on a beach. By their apparel and the look of the photograph, the era was dated to nineteen twenties.

"By traditional standards, yes," said Computer. "However, many Society members choose to wait. As you may recall, Jennifer, no Society member can live under the same roof with an outsider, not even if that outsider is the Member's child. Until that child shows sign and also becomes a member, it must live elsewhere, and remain unaware of the existence of the Society."

"Or... the family can be Grey Caste," said Jennifer.

Matthew climbed off the access ladder and entered the Apartment as Computer and Jennifer continued their conversation. He quietly went into the kitchen.

"That is true," said Computer. "A special status was created approximately twenty years ago that allow Society members to live with non-Society, but only under special circumstances and under very severe restrictions. Such level of Society membership is known as Grey Caste."

"How many Grey Caste are there?" asked Jennifer.

"I do not have the most current information," said Computer. "I will begin the research and attempt to extrapolate an approximate number for you. I am afraid there is a high probability that I will not be able to acquire an exact figure."

"Don't sweat it. Cancel that research; it isn't important."

Matthew came up behind the couch, a can of iced tea in hand.

"Society population, twelve thousand, of which fewer than two hundred are Grey Caste at any one time," he said matter-of-factly. He opened his can of iced tea with a loud pop.

"Geez, Dad." Jennifer jumped, startled. "Where'd you come from?"

Matthew climbed up onto the back of the couch and sat with his feet on the cushions.

"History lesson?"

"All morning. I thought it was time for a review." She settled back. "You hang out with a scary bunch of folks."

"You can't choose your family."

There was an awkward pause, after which Matthew slid down and sat beside Jennifer. She laid her head back.

"Even growing up with this, it all seems way too bizarre. I can study the story of the Society from its very beginnings, and I can make myself believe that it all makes sense. But when I climb up that ladder and go back into the real world, none of it makes sense. None of it seems right. None of it... belongs. We don't belong; up there or down here."

The display showed another photograph of Victor.

"Like it or not, we were born of the Society," said Matthew. "Whether Victor Broderick likes it or not."

"Not," Jennifer stated.

"The Sutherland family was, and is, one of the seventeen Primary Families of the Society." Matthew fell into a calm melancholy. "Whether we like it or not, you and I have to somehow live in both worlds."

After a moment of appropriate silence, Computer spoke up.

"Eleven thousand, three hundred and fifty five."

Matthew glanced up. "What?"

"Society population is eleven thousand, three hundred and fifty five, of which three thousand, two hundred are of the Primary families, the remainder are of the Lesser Families."

"Have you been sulking?" asked Matthew.

"I do not sulk. Your figure of twelve thousand was imprecise."

"I do worry about you."

"There is no need," said Computer. "I continually monitor the status of all my components and perform scheduled diagnostics. Any deviations are corrected and any requiring human interactions are always reported to you in a timely manner."

"Now you're being deliberately obtuse," said Matthew.

Chapter Seven

Victor helped Robby and Thomas out of the large sedan while looking with satisfaction at the grounds and stately buildings of the Academy. They walked from the car and onto the grounds proper, followed the walkway that would take them beneath the great oak tree in the center of the grounds.

"The Academy is a wonderful old institution," Victor said to his children. "While you have attained membership, all members must complete their instruction here prior to attaining full rights."

He indicated a new building off to their right.

"That building over there is the dormitory," he said. "For many, it is easier to stay here on the campus while attending. You of course will be coming home to your mother and me each afternoon."

They passed beneath the tree. Victor saw Mary sitting high up in the branches. He spoke to her using thought talk, mind to mind.

"Good morning, Mary."

There was no immediate response. However, as they continued on toward the Academy main building, her words brushed his mind:

"Good morning."

Victor and his children continued to the administration building, climbed the steps and entered the foyer.

The security guard, a large, broad-shouldered man, was sitting behind a desk. He watched the new arrivals approach.

"Good morning, Father," he said. "The Headmaster is expecting you."

"Thank you, Jim," said Victor.

Victor led his children down the hall. They passed through the outer vestibule and into the Headmaster's office. The Headmaster stood behind his desk, gave a deep nod and waved a hand for Victor and his children to be seated.

"Good morning, Father," said the Headmaster.

"Good morning, Headmaster." Victor sat down, watched his children take their seats. He turned again to the Headmaster. "I saw Mary outside."

"In the tree again?" Headmaster said aloud, continued then in thought talk, mind to mind. "You saw my report?"

"I agree with your assessment," Victor answered in thought talk.

He looked to his children, again to Headmaster, spoke aloud.

"You remember Robby and Thomas?" he asked. "They are very excited about getting started."

"We've talked many times." Headmaster smiled at the children. "So, you are looking forward to beginning your classes, then?"

The children gave obligatory nods and Headmaster turned his attention back to Victor.

"They will do very well here, Father. They are quite bright and very talented."

Headmaster placed his forearms on his desk and his expression grew fixed. He and Victor spoke now in thought talk.

"You've read the details on Mary's signs?"

"I am quite pleased by the reports," Victor sent back.

"You are not concerned?"

"Concerned? Not at all. She may well be everything we hoped for."

"And then some."

"All the better."

"I of course bow to your judgment, Father."

The boys looked first to Victor, then to Headmaster, then back again. They knew there was a conversation going on that they weren't witness to.

Victor looked side-glance at them. He gave them a wink, then spoke aloud to Headmaster.

"Continue to voice your concerns, Headmaster. And by all means, proceed with due caution. Do not, however, attempt to inhibit her growth in any way."

He looked again to the children, smiled broadly.

"I am quite proud of my children. I have no doubts regarding their success at the Academy."

"You may leave them in my care, Father."

"Yes. Yes, of course." Victor showed no indications of leaving.

Headmaster smiled patiently.

"They will be waiting for you when you return for them this afternoon," he said.

"Yes."

It took another few moments for Victor to stand. Headmaster stood then, his expression sympathetic.

"No easier the second time around, is it?" he asked.

"Was I as anxious with the other children?"

"I had quite the time getting you to leave," said the Headmaster.

"Well... I'll not cause a scene this time around." He knelt before the children and spoke warmly to them. "I'll be back this afternoon. And don't forget... the most important thing is to enjoy yourselves. You pay attention to what you are told, and do your best; but do not forget to have fun."

He stood again and looked back to the Headmaster.

"Until this afternoon."

Headmaster watched Victor leave the room, then smiled comfortingly at the children, sitting patiently in their chairs. He sensed both anxiety and anticipation from them.

Good.

Victor came out onto the front steps of the Academy main building. He stopped to admire the view and take in the moment. The sun was shining, the air was fresh and clear. He heard the sound of children laughing somewhere in the distance.

He looked over at the large tree in which he had seen Mary, then took the steps and starting along walk toward the tree.

He reached out to Mary in thought talk while still some distance from the tree.

"Mary?"

There was no response. As he came nearer, he could see that she was still in the branches.

"Good morning to you again, Mary," he sent to her.

He was within a few steps of the tree.

"Good morning, Father," she sent to him, mind-to-mind.

Victor passed under the tree, continued walking.

"And how are you doing?" he asked her. "Are you enjoying your time here?"

"I have no complaints."

"I am very glad to hear that." Victor was getting near his car. "Shouldn't you be in class?"

"I am in class."

"I see," said Victor. "I do like your classroom. But I recall that mornings are usually devoted to more traditional activity; reading, writing, arithmetic."

"I am special."

Victor smiled to himself, though he suspected she could sense that. He reached his car. There was a moment of silence.

"Father... would you like me to keep an eye on your children?"

"Thank you, Mary. I would be honored."

There was a pallet of bricks sitting on the walkway. Matthew was on his knees in front of a partially completed retaining wall that bordered the walk and enclosed a raised flowerbed.

It was another nice day, but there were clouds on the horizon.

Sam came up with a wheelbarrow load of prepared mortar mix. Matthew looked in the wheelbarrow, pushed a trowel into the mixture.

"It looks good, Sam."

"You really ought to get a mixer," said Sam.

Matthew gave Sam a devilish grin, turned back to his work without responding.

"Yeah, yeah... I know," Sam sighed. "You already have one."

"It's good for you," said Matthew.

Jennifer came down the walkway from the direction of the front of the house. Sam turned his attention to her. Seeing Sam's distraction, Matthew turned his head enough to see his daughter coming.

He gave a knowing glance to Sam, returned to his work.

Jennifer looked vaguely perturbed at Sam's presence.

"Hello, Sam."

"Hi, Jen." Sam indicated their work. "What do you think?"

"Not bad." She looked to her father then. "Are you going to run it all the way down the walk?"

"I'll enclose this bed." He used the trowel to point to the other side of the walkway. "Can't make up my mind about the other side, though."

Sam spoke up: "I told him he should do the same to both sides of the walk."

Jennifer studied the walkway, trying to give her father's dilemma the attention it deserved.

"Yeah, well, you know my dad," she said. "Once he's built, planted or grown something, why do it again." She indicated the grounds all about them. "These grounds are testimony to his 'now let's try it this way' philosophy."

"I like it here," said Sam.

"I know." Jennifer folded her arms across her chest, turned her attention back to her father. "How much longer are you going to be, Dad?"

Matthew didn't miss a beat, continued working.

"Something up?" he asked.

"Nothing that can't wait a few minutes." She glanced up, away, to the house. "Some info has come in on one of the projects we've been working on."

"Right. Let me get through this last batch of mortar. I'll be in once we get things cleaned up."

Sam took a look at the approaching clouds. They looked dark.

"We should cover this wall in plastic, Mr. Sutherland. It looks like it might rain later."

"Good man, Sam," said Matthew. "See what you can find in the shed."

Sam hesitated. He knew that Jennifer would be gone when he got back.

She made it easy for him by turning and returning to the front of the house. At that, Sam headed to the shed in the yard at the back of the house.

Matthew looked to his left and then his right at the receding figures of Sam and Jennifer. He allowed himself a chuckle, as if he had somehow done something.

Chapter Eight

Matthew stepped off the ladder, walked across the Apartment and stood beside Jennifer, before the wall display.

"Computer has more info on Andover," said Jennifer.

"Give it to me, Computer," said Matthew.

"Please specify, Matthew."

Matthew rubbed his forehead, his temple.

"You know what I'm asking, Computer. It's not like you weren't listening."

There was a long, awkward silence. Matthew waited for Computer to begin the review, Jennifer watched Matthew grow more impatient, and Computer stubbornly waited for Matthew to be more specific.

Matthew finally surrendered.

"Computer. Jennifer tells me that you have more information regarding the Andover situation. When you have a moment, will you fill us in?"

"It is one of my functions, Matthew."

"It certainly is."

The display wall before them lit up with a photograph of Carlson, the mayor of Andover. The picture moved to one side, making room for a data window of text.

The display lasted for several seconds, after which the photo and text disappeared, to be replaced with a photograph of Robert Addison, which slid to one side, making room for its data window of text.

Computer spoke as these and then additional displays came and went.

"The fabricated pasts of the Society members in Andover are quite thorough. There completed life histories for each of them."

"I'm sure that didn't slow you down much," said Matthew. "You've ID'd them?"

"All have been identified."

"Good work."

"Thank you, Matthew," said Computer. "Each new arrival in Andover coincided with the disappearance of a

Society member elsewhere, sometimes to within several weeks."

"Then it should have been fairly easy for you, shouldn't it?"

"Once my research made a connection between the disappearance in one location and an appearance in Andover, it was not difficult to make a positive match."

Matthew looked side glance to Jennifer.

"Computer keeps track of as many Members as he can, but it's impossible to always know where every individual is at any given moment. When one drops out of sight and doesn't surface again..." he leaned near his daughter and whispered, "... it drives him a little batty."

Matthew was sitting on the couch, looking up at the wall display. It was showing a photograph of the street intersection in Andover that made up the downtown.

Jennifer was standing behind the couch, leaning back against it, facing away from the display.

"It will be just a quick trip," said Matthew.

"To do what?" asked Jennifer. She folded her arms, stared down at her feet. "We still don't have any idea what it's all about."

"Exactly."

Jennifer shook her head, pushed off the couch, turned around and climbed onto the back of the couch.

"Then what good will it do? Dad, we need to get more info before we start poking our noses around up there."

"I gotta see what the fuss is about."

"Then I'll go with you."

"It's a simple recon." Matthew shifted on the couch to face Jennifer. "I'll be in and out of there in a day. Better if you're here to keep Computer from getting lazy. You said yourself—we need more info. You stay here and keep digging."

"Am I in the Family Business or not?"

"Up to your armpits. Don't you worry. There will be ample opportunity for you to risk your neck. First Recon is a one-person job. This time out, that's me."

Jennifer frowned, slid down from the back of the couch to the seat.

"Yeah, well, I don't like it."

"Neither did your mother."

Chapter Nine

Matthew guided his pickup alongside the pumps at the Andover Quickstop, stopped and turned off the engine. He climbed out and moved to the pump. He took in the community as he filled the tank.

The downtown area consisted of a handful of retail storefronts and a long building housing the town hall, police station, mayor's office and volunteer fire house.

The scene was a strange mix of the normal and the surreal, everyday sights and sounds filtered through an ethereal haze.

A police car pulled up along the other side of the pumps and the police chief climbed out and began pumping gas. He glanced warily at Matthew. There was a visible air of barely suppressed enmity in the way he looked at this stranger to his town.

The gas nozzle clicked off. Matthew returned it to the pump, put the gas cap back on, and walked to the open door of the store.

A young woman stood behind the counter near the register. Matthew got in line behind two men and a woman. The two men stepped up to the counter together.

"Hey, Meg," said one. "Give me the chicken and Jo-Jos."

"Me too," said the other. They were on a lunch break from the mill.

"You got it." Meg moved to one side to put together the baskets.

The first man leaned a hip against the counter and frowned.

"Man, I don't wanna go back in there today."

"What do you got to whine about, Carl?" said the second. "All you do is sit up there and bitch all day. You don't do a damn thing."

"Yeah? Like you got it so tough."

"I'm not the one doin' the whining."

"Yeah?" Carl tried to hide a grin. "How 'bout I kick your ass? We'll see some whining, then."

"Don't tire yourself."

Meg brought the two baskets over, started to ring up the totals. Carl put a bill on the counter.

"I got 'em, Meg," he said.

"Thank you, Carl." She picked up the money, opened the register and put the bill into the slot.

The police chief came into the store, stood in line behind Matthew. There was a sudden, definite change in the air; a heavy silence, though no one outwardly acted any differently.

Carl and his buddy picked up their lunch baskets and started toward the door.

"I say we grab a coupla' beers to go with these and head in the opposite direction," said Carl.

"Sounds great," the other said doubtfully. "And do what?"

"Anything. Anything we want."

"Yeah... you gotta give me more than that."

Outside, they started across the parking lot and in the direction of the mill.

The line at the counter moved forward and the woman put her few things on the counter.

"Is this it for you, Angie?" asked Meg.

"All for today, Meg."

Meg rang up the items and began putting them into a bag.

"Nine forty," she said.

Angela handed Meg a ten dollar bill. Meg looked past Angela and Matthew to the police chief as she gave Angela her change. Angela smiled uncomfortably as she quickly gathered her things.

"Thank you," she said. She started toward the door.

Matthew moved up to the counter, pulled his wallet out and held it ready. The police chief was close behind him.

"Welcome to Andover," said Meg. She seemed distracted.

"Thank you," said Matthew. "Pump one."

"Anything else?"

"Just the gas, thanks."

"Eighteen even," said Meg, not looking at the pump register.

Matthew pulled out eighteen dollars. Handing it to Meg, he glanced back over his shoulder. The police chief stood silent, looking directly at him.

Matthew turned back to Meg.

"Where's a good place for a sit-down lunch?" he asked.

There was a long moment of heavy quiet when nothing appeared to happen.

"Sally's," Meg said at last. "Right around the corner."

"Thank you." Matthew moved away from the counter.

"Sure thing. Come again."

Matthew started away from the counter, hesitated as he reached the door. Looking back into the store, the police chief hadn't moved to the counter, was watching him. Meg, her hands resting on the counter, managed a smile in Matthew's direction.

"Thanks, Meg," said Matthew. "I'll do that."

Matthew turned the pickup into an available parking space in front of Sally's Café, a low structure with a flat roof, a wall of windows with the front door at one end of the building. He took a leisurely look around before slowly walking to the door.

The café was two-thirds full. Jan, the waitress, approached and directed Matthew to an open booth.

Robert Addison and his wife Linda were in the booth next to his. Robert watched Jan fill the stranger's water glass and take his order.

"Carlson's right," Robert said in thought talk. "It's him."

"Probably," Linda sent back, mind-to-mind.

"It's him," Robert returned. "Did you see the way he took in the room? He picked out every Member here, almost instantly. Who else could do that?"

Daniel and Emma Chandler came into the café. Robert watched as Matthew quickly took in the Chandlers, then appeared to ignore them.

"Daniel! Emma!" Jan said, took a step toward them. She called back in the direction of the kitchen. "Sally! Come out here!"

Sally, a middle-aged woman dressed in black slacks and a brightly colored blouse, came out from the back to greet

them. Robert divided his attention between Matthew sitting
in his booth and Sally greeting the Chandlers.

"Did you see how he reacted to the Chandlers coming
in?" Robert sent to his wife.

"No, I'm sorry. Not really," Linda said aloud, in a low
voice.

Matthew was absently watching Sally talking with the
Chandler's at their booth when Jan came with Matthew's
lunch of burger, fries and iced tea. While not overly friendly,
Jan was polite enough.

"Will there be anything else?" she asked.

"Not just now. Thanks."

"Enjoy your lunch," she said, starting away.

Matthew took a bite of his hamburger, munched on a
couple of fries. He took his time. As he ate, he listened.

In addition to the normal sounds of people at lunch,
there was something else; an undercurrent of sound. There
was a noise, a hissing sound of thoughts and words, all just
under the surface. Matthew was able to snatch a word here
and there.

He casually glanced at the Addisons in the next booth.
He caught Robert glaring at him before he slowly turned
away.

Matthew continued eating, observing... and listening.

Robert turned his head, slowly, until he was looking
directly at Matthew. He reached down and took hold of
Linda's hand. She looked at him, then looked around the
room.

There were occasional bursts of static in the
background. The subvocal whispers grew suddenly louder...
then stopped.

Robert continued looking at Matthew. He watched
Matthew slowly put down his hamburger and take a drink of
his iced tea.

There were several sudden, flashing images of Matthew's
past, pictures of Matthew Sutherland: with his daughter,

with Computer, with his vehicles, with Sam; with Sharon, his wife.

Sudden, rushing close-up of Matthew's face Present Time; a barely perceptible movement of his eyes. At that instant, Robert was visibly thrown back into his seat.

Linda and several others turned quickly and looked at Robert; Robert sat stunned.

"Did you see that?" He asked aloud, a harsh whisper. "Did you feel that? He did that on his own!"

Matthew calmly finished his hamburger.

The subvocal hissing whispers continued to intensify. Matthew caught quick words of violence among the static.

He finished his French fries, took another drink from his iced tea.

He caught then, very clearly, Robert saying subvocally: "We should kill him now."

Matthew calmly took another drink from his iced tea.

Chapter Ten

Jennifer came from the back of the main house, turning off lights along the way. Coming into the foyer, she made sure the front door was locked. She glanced out the window before heading down the hall toward the door to the basement.

She worked her way down to the Apartment. The room was quiet but for the faint hum of the computer equipment.

"Any word, Computer?"

"Your father left Andover thirty five minutes ago," said Computer. "He should be checking into the hotel in Olympia within the hour."

Jennifer slid onto the couch, pulled her feet up and wrapped her arms comfortably around her legs.

"Why didn't you tell me?"

"I am not permitted to communicate with you while you are upstairs unless there is an emergency or I am specifically directed to do so. I monitor the grounds for intrusion or other danger, but am programmed to disregard all personal—"

"Stop," Jennifer cut him off. "Ya' know, I think there's a lot more going on in those vacuum tubes of yours than you let on."

"As you are well aware, Jennifer, vacuum tubes have not been used in the manufacture of compu—"

"I know that."

There was a long pause. Both were silent.

"And you know that I know that," said Jennifer. Another pause. "Computer?"

"Yes, Jennifer?"

"You always know the right thing to say."

"It is the way Matthew programmed me."

"Sure." Jennifer smiled nostalgically. "You and I have both done some growing since then."

"Yes, Jennifer," Computer stated matter-of-factly. Several moments later then: "Upon his departure from Andover, Matthew stated that all went well. He will be making a full report once he checks into his room."

"Anything else?"

"He asked how you were."

"You can tell him that I'm all alone in a hole in the ground, getting ready to eat leftovers."

"Sensors indicate that Matthew is no longer in the vehicle. I will attempt to deliver your message when—"

"Stop toying with me."

"Jennifer, I—"

"He's out of the pickup?"

"The sensor indicates that no one is in the vehicle."

"How long ago?"

"I cancelled constant monitoring of that sensor once Matthew left the Andover community, whereupon I returned to intermittent check mode," said Computer. "I sought current sensor status immediately prior to attempting to deliver your message."

"Then he must be—"

"Excuse me, Jennifer. Matthew's John Marshall credit card has just been used to register into the hotel."

Jennifer let out a sigh of relief. Computer continued.

"John Marshall is the identity selected to indicate that all is well and that there is no duress."

"I need something to eat," said Jennifer.

She stood and went to the kitchen. Opening the refrigerator, she brought out a bowl of leftovers, shook her head in bewilderment.

"If there hadn't been computers, Dad would have had to invent them," she said. "There's no way he could have played these games without you to keep track of all this crap."

Computer responded calmly and without emotion, as always.

"I keep your father alive."

Jennifer was numbed by the statement. She stood before the microwave, bowl in hand.

The silence hung heavy in the air.

"Matthew has made Internet contact," said Computer. "Report begins."

§

The hotel room was clean, comfortable, but nothing special. Matthew was sitting at the desk. The report finished, he turned off his laptop. He stared at the darkening display a moment, then slid the chair back and stood up.

He walked across the room, leaned a shoulder tiredly against the wall beside the draped window; he looked absently back into the room; something was brushing at his mind; something nearby... something... bad.

Outside, the night was dark, wet. Across the narrow parking lot, Robert Addison was sitting on the hood of a car. He appeared calm, his feet on the bumper, elbows on his knees and hands clasped.

Victor's home office was lit only by a single lamp. Victor was sitting at his desk, a photograph in his hand. It showed Matthew Sutherland standing in line at the counter in the Andover Quickstop.

He tossed the picture onto the desk. He rubbed his face with his hands, turned his chair until he was facing the dark window.

"Damn," he grumbled.

Dianna was standing in the doorway, little more than a silhouette.

"What does he know?" she asked.

"Enough." Victor turned about his chair and pulled the photograph to him. He stared at it, frowning. He pushed it aside again. "His way of letting us know that he's onto us. But it was recon. He knows we're up to something, but not what or why."

"Victor..." She moved into the room.

"Damn him."

"This project is too important to let Matthew—"

"Yes, yes," Victor said irritably. He turned away from Dianna. "As Father, my first duty is to protect the Society. My second duty is to the prosperity of the members of the Society." He turned back. "By inference, my third duty is to ensure the survival of the Andover project."

"He has left you with no alternative."

"For decades, he has been little more than a thorn in my side, never really a serious threat. Lately..."

"If only—"

"Yes," said Victor. "When Sharon..."

"What else could we do?"

"I know. And now..." Victor rested his head against the back of the chair. "That damnable computer creation of his. If anything happens to him or his daughter, everything they know about the Society will be sent out to dozens of news organizations around the world."

"So, what do we do, Victor?"

"As you said, we have no choice. And the longer we delay, the more difficult it will be. It's obvious that his daughter is being groomed to join the family business." He let out a tired sigh. "How did we come to this?"

"You can't blame yourself, my love," said Dianna. "You have done everything possible to avoid what Matthew has made inevitable."

Chapter Eleven

The Andover Elementary School was little more than a handful of administration offices, a row of classrooms, and the auditorium, which also served as cafeteria and school gym.

There were eight cars in the small parking lot. To the east, the horizon was just beginning to turn a predawn pink.

A ninth car pulled into the lot. Daniel Chandler and his wife Emma got out, walked across the lot and approached the front doors.

The police chief stood in the foyer. The Chandlers said nothing as they passed him.

There were several dozen people in the auditorium, gathered in groups of three and four. Some were talking aloud, others subvocally using thought talk.

The mayor was in deep conversation with Linda Addison, Meg and Angela. Linda looked anxious, yet excited. When the mayor saw the Chandlers enter the auditorium, he waved them over to join them.

"Welcome," he said, shaking Daniel's hand.

"Good evening, Mayor," said Daniel.

"Hello, Tom," said Emma.

Daniel quickly scanned the room, looked briefly at each of those gathered. He turned again to the mayor, spoke to the entire group.

"I'm glad to see that Victor has finally decided to put an end to the Sutherland problem."

Meg and Angela bristled at the comment. The mayor, however, maintained his vague political face.

"It had to have been a difficult decision for Father to make, Dan."

"Quite," Emma agreed. "Everyone knows how close Victor and Matthew once were."

"Everyone also knows the threat that he poses to the Society," said Daniel.

Linda Addison pushed aside her anxiety.

"He shall be dealt with tonight," she said.

"We all hope so," said Daniel.

"No time for doubts, my friend," said Mayor Carlson.

"Matthew Sutherland is not a threat to be dealt with lightly."

"We were recently witness to that," agreed Emma.

Linda gave a sharp, sure nod.

"We will not be caught unawares again, Emma," she said.

Emma gave Linda a faint smile, spoke with a barely hidden patronizing tone.

"Of course not," she said.

"Robert is not totally without his own strengths," said Linda. "With mine to support him, and through me all over yours, Matthew Sutherland will not be a problem."

Meg stepped into the conversation for the first time.

"What about that AI of his?" she asked.

The mayor responded with an air of authority.

"The Father will make contact with it the moment Matthew has been dealt with. A truce will be offered— Jennifer will remain unharmed so long as the computer does not release Society information."

Daniel nodded agreement, "Victor is certain that Matthew has made his daughter's safety the computer's number one directive."

"Once the truce is made," said the mayor, "we will have all the time we need to complete the Andover project and find a way to deal with Jennifer Sutherland and the threat the Sutherland computer holds over us."

The police chief came into the auditorium then, ceremoniously closed the doors behind him. It took several moments for the room to grow quiet, during which time everyone in the room grew introspective.

Linda Addison wound her way through the people and into the middle of the room. The others in the room began to drift toward her. She calmly and unhurriedly turned about in a circle and stopped. She moved her feet apart, held her arms slightly out, palms out.

She closed her eyes...

§

Robert Addison slid off the hood, stood beside his car. He looked over the hood to the hotel, outside room doors even spaced, alternating with large, draped windows. Behind him, a wall of trees bordered the parking lot.

He took a long, deep breath.

He closed his eyes...

In the Andover Elementary auditorium, Linda smiled. She breathed deep, moved her arms further away from her body.

She made contact.

Eight people in the auditorium formed a circle around her. Holding their arms out, their hands just touched. As others in the auditorium began closing in around the circle, the eight laid their heads back and closed their eyes.

In the hotel parking lot, Robert Addison took in strength, swallowed energy.

An old neighborhood in Andover, just before dawn; it was wet outside.

A middle-aged woman came out onto her porch. Next door, another stepped outside, onto her porch.

Half a dozen homes, half a century old... neighbors came out onto their porches. They looked up into the predawn sky. They spread their arms, hands, palms out.

They closed their eyes...

In the auditorium, those outside the circle of eight had formed a larger outer circle.

In the parking lot, Robert Addison moved away from the car.

Matthew stood in the middle of his hotel room. The only light was that leaking in from around the sides of the drapes, sending shadows across Matthew's face and frame.

He gave a glance to his laptop, which was still sitting on the desk across the room. With the casual flick of two of his fingers, the display shattered and whorls of smoke came up through the keys.

He went to the door, opened it and stepped outside.

Arms loose at his sides, he twitched a finger. The door closed behind him.

There were seven vehicles in the lot, including his pickup. The predawn air was wet, the asphalt and cars shimmering with the damp.

Robert Addison was standing near the treeline bordering the parking lot.

Matthew took a step from the porch of his hotel room.

Suddenly then the parking lot, the hotel, the surrounding world... all spun dizzily... all went fuzzy...

The world cleared then, refocused; the hotel, the parking lot.

Robert Addison was looking down the treeline... to where Matthew now stood, some forty feet away.

They eyed each other, studied each other...

Robert twitched a hand, almost imperceptibly. The large tree beside him ripped from the soil, uprooted, and was tossed toward Matthew.

With a tilt of the head, Matthew shattered the tree in midair. A thousand large splinters rained onto the parking lot.

Five of the largest splinters lifted up from the asphalt and rushed at Matthew.

He casually lifted a hand. The wood exploded into a cloud of powder in front of him.

He tilted his head, twitched. Six medium sized trees, still standing upright, rushed toward Robert, surrounded him, closed in tightly around him.

Robert flicked two fingers. The trees exploded into thick chunks of sawdust, leaving Robert standing unharmed in the dusty cloud.

In the elementary school auditorium, Linda was standing inside the circle of eight, the larger circle beyond. Her hair was limp, her skin shiny and pasty. Her arms trembled slightly.

On the porches of the old neighborhood, men and women stood unmoving, arms out, hands out, heads back with eyes closed; faces pasty, hair hanging damp.

§

Robert turned his head, looked back to his car. He spun his head back then. The car lifted off the ground, turned on its side and rushed at Matthew.

Matthew looked at the car and the metal of the vehicle was crushed in midair. The car spun about and rushed back toward Robert.

Robert swung his arm and the car was flung back into the parking lot, crashing down onto its wheels.

Matthew took the moment to look sharply at Robert. Robert was pushed violently back, as if from a blow. He stumbled but remained standing.

In the auditorium, Linda's eyes opened wide and she sucked in a throaty breath.

On a porch in the old neighborhood, a middle-aged woman fell to her knees, clutched at her chest. She reached out to the porch rail, her face taut with surprise and pain.

In the auditorium, tears ran down Linda's cheek.

She was suddenly afraid.

Matthew took a step nearer Robert, then another. He ignored the trees and cars. He focused on Robert.

Robert cried out in pain. He twisted in distress. He tried to fight back, but Matthew easily tossed the attempts aside. Matthew took another step, and another, moved methodically closer to Robert. Robert shuddered at every slight twitch or flick from Matthew.

Robert fell to his knees.

Matthew took a final step, six feet from Robert. Matthew's expression was calm but determined.

Robert let out a piercing mind scream.

In the elementary school auditorium, Linda fell to her knees and let out her own mind scream. Those around her were thrown violently backward, some stumbling to remain standing, many thrown hard to the hardwood floor.

On the porches of the old neighborhood, neighbors thrown back against the wall fell to their knees, fell forward.

Matthew looked away from Robert Addison's body. He started across the parking lot. The debris that littered the lot moved out of his path as he walked to his pickup. Debris that covered his pickup was thrown clear.

He climbed in behind the wheel.

There was a clear path out of the parking lot.

Victor stood at the window, gray early morning light glowing dully on his face. It streamed past him and into the room, his office in heavy shadow.

He turned to his wife, standing in middle of the room. She held her arms stiffly at her sides, a look of desperation on her face that she tried to hide with a false calm reassurance.

Something bad had happened. They both sensed it, felt it.

Victor set his own expression...

He was Father.

They would overcome whatever was out there.

He turned back to the window, clasped his hands behind his back.

Mary was sitting in the wooden chair in the middle of her small room. She was looking in the direction of her window. The curtain was pulled aside, the gray light of early morning streaming in.

While there was a calmness in her expression, there was little emotion visible on her young face

Chapter Twelve

The lights of the Apartment were set to dim, the glow from the rows of active security monitors pushing into the middle of the room. Matthew was sitting at the kitchen counter, his back to the room, absently dunking a tea bag in a cup of hot water.

Jennifer stepped off the access ladder and into the room. She walked across the room and came up behind Matthew. She hugged her father about the shoulders, moved around beside him and climbed onto the empty stool next to him.

"Feeling any better?" she asked.

"I'm fine," said Matthew.

Jennifer nodded slowly, not completely convinced, but decided to let it go.

"Sam came by today," she said. "Looking for you."

Matthew lifted the tea bag out and set it on the saucer.

"He's a good kid," he said.

"Uh, huh."

"What time is it?" He rubbed at his tired eyes.

"About eleven thirty."

"Night?"

"Uh, huh."

"Damn." He turned and slid off the stool.

He reached back, picked up his cup of tea and carried it over to the table. He sat down and leaned back in the chair.

Jennifer followed and sat in the chair opposite. She studied him a moment.

"Well?" she finally asked.

Matthew looked up, looked across the table to his daughter. Their eyes locked and each seemed to be searching out the other. He finally leaned forward, however hesitantly, and set the cup of tea on the table.

"Everyone was watching, Jen," he said. "Everyone. Pushing. I wasn't fighting just Addison. I was fighting the whole town. They were... feeding him."

"I've never heard of that," said Jennifer. "I mean, I've heard of linking, but it's always one member supporting another; never a group."

"Me either. A few with the ability to support, like Addison's wife." Matthew frowned. "This was more. She... funneled. Like a conduit. I was facing all of them; from all over Andover."

Jennifer reached out and rested a hand on her father's forearm.

"And you won."

"I don't think we won anything."

"I don't understand."

Matthew leaned back again, spoke into the air.

"Computer," he said. "Update, please."

"Andover population is eighty three percent evacuated," said Computer.

"Current location of evacuees?"

"Unknown."

Matthew turned again to Jennifer.

"They began leaving almost immediately; most likely following a pre-established emergency plan."

"So you won," Jennifer stated again. "Whatever they were planning, it's not happening."

"Delayed, maybe," he said, sighing. "And we don't know what *it* is. We have no idea what their goal was for Andover, or if this funneling had any part in it."

"We know that you have the strength to stand against a whole town."

Matthew shook his head and leaned further forward.

"Nope. That's just one more question," he said. "It shouldn't have been possible. Not even close."

Jennifer had no response to that. She knew that he was right. There was no way her father should have been able to take on an entire town, whatever the inherent strength of his Abilities.

"We can assume the few folks remaining in Andover are not Society," she said, redirecting the conversation. "They have to be confused right about now. And there are going to be a few stories hitting the wires."

"So true."

"We can also assume that Computer will be in Batty Mode for the next few weeks, looking for signs of where our Andover refugees went."

"Also true." Matthew reached out and picked up his tea. He took a sip. It was already getting cold.

He set the cup back on the table, pushed it aside.

"Let's put ourselves in Victor's shoes," said Jennifer. "We may not know the goal they've set for themselves, but we may be able to extrapolate what Victor's next step might be."

"Maybe." Matthew leaned back, fought back a yawn. "But not tonight."

Victor climbed out of his car, looked up into the sunny sky as he gently closed the door. He turned about then and started across the Academy grounds, following the winding concrete walk. He slowed as he reached the great Oak tree, stopped once he was beneath its wide branches.

He stepped up to the gnarly trunk, leaned against the bark.

He spoke aloud, without looking up into canopy.

"You were there," he said.

Mary didn't respond at first.

"I was," she said finally, also speaking aloud.

"Mary..." he started. "Why did you help him?"

"I did very little."

"It was enough."

"Yes," she said. "I had no choice."

"That isn't true," said Victor. "You had a choice. You could have stayed out of it."

Mary said nothing.

"I thought we were friends, Mary."

"The Society must come first, Father."

"Always," said Victor. "Absolutely."

"Everything that happened, had to happen."

"Your Sight is not developed, Mary," said Victor, frowning and shaking his head. "It is untrained. Taking actions on it now is dangerous."

"I know what I know."

"And what is it that you know?" Victor asked. "Must Matthew live in order for the Society to survive?"

"No."

"Then what? We have been set back months, maybe years. Is that a good thing?"

Mary hesitated.

"What happened, had to happen," she said then, pretty much repeating what she had said a moment before.

Victor pushed away from the tree and started slowly away.

He spoke to her then in thought talk, mind-to-mind.

"Perhaps the next time you choose to side against us, you can do me the honor of letting me know."

Up in the tree, Mary turned her head and glanced up, glanced away.

"If it serves the Society to do so," she sent, mind to mind.

Mary turned her face to the sun, closed her eyes. She let the warmth of the rays soothe her.

The 64 Comet was parked in the small lot of Rydel Ridge. Matthew was sitting on the hood, leaning back on the windshield, eyes closed.

He was taking in the same sun as young Mary.

End Episode One...

Shadows from the Past
Short Stories Collection

Introduction

Most of my short stories have been lost, particularly those written using my old typewriter back before I had a computer, and more than a few written with only pencil and paper. But I did manage to hang onto a couple from way back when.

Included here are a handful I managed to hang onto...

Yesterday's Shadows
Written about 1975, heavy on TZ influence

Reunions
First published in Necrology Magazine, Tales of Macabre

Last Day at Sharp Park
Written in 1971, when I was fifteen years old.

The Light in the Mist
A Victorian Fairie Tale (well, sort of...)

Room
The assignment was to write a "white room" story...

Note:
These five titles have appeared in earlier collections and publications.

Yesterday's Shadows

Introduction

This was written sometime around 1975, so I was about eighteen or nineteen years old at the time. It begins as an Outer Limits kind of post-disaster tale and then takes a left turn into the Twilight Zone. I'm certain I had no idea of the influence of these programs at the time I was writing it, but in reading it now, that influence is obvious.

Yesterday's Shadows

The sun would be setting soon. Time to find a place to spend the night.

Peter took his steps cautiously, walking down the center of the street, carefully examining each house that he passed. They stared back emptily, their windows dull and gray; most had their curtains drawn.

There were no sounds but that of his own footsteps echoing out ahead of him.

He watched for any sign of movement, anything to show that his presence had caught someone's attention. Anything... a shadow falling across a window, a door slowly and silently closing, a curtain falling back into place. But there was nothing. If there was anyone here, they were too weak or too frightened to show themselves, even guardedly. If anyone watched, hidden away in the dark, from behind those dark, dusty drapes, they would rather this man pass by, leave them alone to their few remaining days.

Slow and steady. Walk with confidence. You are strong and healthy and unafraid. You can take on anything and anyone...

What the hell am I doing out in the middle of the street?

Gotta find a place for the night...

Peter stepped onto the sidewalk and stopped in front of the very next house. This would do. A nice little place. Pleasant, modest, warm atmosphere. Brown stucco. He liked the short hedge that lined the walk leading up to the porch. The lawn was dry and showing signs of neglect, but that was to be expected, wasn't it? What with everything that had happened over the last six months.

Peter walked up to the front door as if he owned the place. The sun, low on the horizon, moved from behind a narrow band of clouds and shown on the door and the large front window. He turned with a final glance up and down the street, at the windows of the row of houses that faced this one. Not a creature was stirring...

The door was locked. He stepped off the porch and walked around to the side of the house, was about to break a window when he found one unlocked.

He climbed into the bedroom that had belonged to a young boy. There was a cute bedspread, about a hundred toys sitting on plastic shelves, almost as many more strewn about on the floor. There were little-boy clothes on the floor beside the bed, and posters hanging on the walls advertised fantasy movies that had premiered long before the little boy was born.

Peter stopped in the hallway, felt for the bulge in the pocket of his jacket. He had quit carrying the rifle several months ago, but had decided to keep the pistol. In all the time he had carried the rifle, he had only fired it once, and he had missed.

True, he had been in situations where perhaps someone else might have used it, but he hadn't been able to bring himself to kill someone as desperate as those that he had come across. If it actually came down to *him or me*, he had no doubts about what he could do, but up to now he had always been able to back out of such situations gracefully. Finally, one day, he just didn't pick up the rifle when he moved on and had yet to have cause to get another one.

Peter let the small backpack slip down to the floor, pulled the pistol from his pocket, let his arms hang loose at his sides. He searched the other bedrooms and bathroom. He noticed the bed in the master bedroom wasn't made. The odor in the bathroom told him that someone had used the toilet after the plumbing had gone out, and he quickly closed the door.

He closed the bedroom doors as he walked back towards the front of the house. The living room looked neat and orderly. The drapes at the windows were thin and let in what little sunlight remained. Several books and magazines were set out on the coffee table and end tables.

"Honey," he called out cynically. "I'm home..."

Stepping into the kitchen, he stopped abruptly, in mid-stride and took a half-step back. His heart seemed to hold its last beat; his breath caught in his throat.

"Hello, *dear*," said the woman.

It took several moments, but Peter managed to let go the breath, if somewhat shakily.

"Hi," he said.

The woman was sitting at the kitchen table, sipping something out of a coffee cup. She wasn't looking at Peter, but staring off into space as if in thought.

"Who are you?" he finally managed to ask. *A stupid thing to ask...*

The woman set the cup down onto the saucer. It gave off a light *chink* sound. She turned her head then and looked at Peter. For several long moments she stared silently. He began to think she wasn't going to say anything.

"Anna," she said at last. "Who are you?"

Peter realized that he was still holding the pistol. He quickly stuffed it back into his jacket pocket. "Peter," he said clumsily. "I'm Peter."

"Have a seat, Peter." Anna picked up the coffee cup. She was trying a little too hard at this *family in the suburbs* thing.

Peter walked over to the counter and leaned against it. "This your house?"

"I was here before you."

Peter shrugged. "Okay... I guess I can find somewhere else to stay."

"Yes," she said stiffly. "I shouldn't think that would be too difficult."

The warm welcome of a few moments before had now hit a definite sour note. Was she intentionally trying to keep him off balance? It wouldn't be hard to do, and he certainly couldn't blame her. Someone in her position, in times like these, could fall prey to any number of dangers. When she looked up at him, an intensity in her eyes forced Peter to turn away. The cupboard doors were inset with glass panes, and he could see the dishes and canned goods inside.

"I suppose not," he said. Looking side-glance, and then turning back again, he watched her carefully set the cup down. She was probably in her late twenties, maybe thirty. She had thick, dark hair, combed and neat. She wore clean jeans and a heavy shirt. Hard to tell, but Peter suspected that she had a nice figure. Her face was attractive, and she still had a healthy look about her. He sensed that she knew he was staring and so turned to look out the window.

Anna brought her elbows up onto the table and rested her chin in one cupped palm. "I have several jugs of water in the cupboard there behind you," she said. "There's some drink mix in the other."

"Thanks." Peter was glad of the opportunity to do something other than stand about looking like an idiot. Even so, he almost dropped the plastic jug and managed to spill as much iced tea mix onto the counter as he put into the glass. Anna opened a can of peaches and served up two bowls, set them on the table. The cupboards were well stocked with a wide variety of canned and boxed foods, which meant that Anna probably planned on staying for a while.

They ate quietly for several minutes, each glancing at the other when one thought the other wasn't looking. Peter finished off his bowl of fruit, set it aside and took another long drink of the tea.

"Have you been here long?" he asked.

"A couple of weeks."

"And you plan on staying," he stated flatly.

"Plan on it, yes."

Peter looked into her eyes and managed this time not to turn away. "What stage are you in?" he asked her.

"Rather blunt," she said. "Six. Maybe Five by now. I'm not sure."

"Can't be Five. There'd be more sign."

"It's hard to tell when you're alone. You can't trust what you see or feel."

"I've had a few doubts."

Anna leaned back in her chair. She seemed a little more comfortable than before. As for himself, Peter saw the mist clearing. He called it the *mist*. When you are alone, there is a hum in the silence that forms a mist in your mind. Only another human voice can burn it away. Anna's voice was soft and he liked the sound of it.

"You can't be more than Stage Seven," she said.

"Coming on Six soon, I think."

Anna nodded slowly; a film covered her eyes. "Not many left at Seven."

"Just me," he agreed.

"Do you realize that by the time you reach Stage One, you'll probably be the only person left alive?" she asked. "On the whole planet..."

Pleasant kitchen table conversation, thought Peter. *Yes, he did realize that...*

"Should make you feel kind of special, don't you think?" Anna leaned forward, reached out, almost took Peter's hand, but stopped just short. She stared absently at her own. "You'll be the last man on Earth. The very last. Then... after that..." Her voice went dead.

Peter pulled back, stood and nervously put his bowl in the sink. *Does she wash the dishes or just throw them out into the yard?*

"I'm sure there are healthy people out there," he said. "Somewhere. Some people are probably immune. And I'm sure some of the important people managed to hide away somewhere safe."

"No one got away," she said. "No one knew it was here until it was too late. Oh, they hid away once they realized how serious it really was, but by then we had all been breathing it in for weeks, or months. No one knew about it. No one suspected." She paused and the silence hurt. Peter came back to the table and sat down, hands folded in his lap. When Anna spoke again, she was vague and distant. She had probably said all this to herself a thousand times before. There would have been no one else around to listen. "Animals started dying, people started dying, and everyone said, *'my, my, what could it be?'*, and then more people died and then everyone started pointing fingers, saying *'it's his fault'* or *'it's their fault'*. And more people died. Then a few stood up, looked around and said *'my, my, look at how many people have died'*."

Her voice had gone low and soft, until Peter could hardly hear her, until it faded and finally died. They sat in silence.

"No one is immune," she said suddenly. "It's in all of us and we are all going to die. There are doctors out there, still alive, still working on it, but they've only been at it a couple of months, and even if they are only at Stage Seven, like you, they only have a couple of months left. Like you. When they die, whatever little they have managed to learn will go with them. But that won't matter. Because there won't be anyone left to pick up where they left off. No one left to save."

He knew that she was probably right. Just a few weeks earlier, he had been near Los Angeles. The stench wouldn't let him get any nearer than a few miles. At one time, bodies were gathered and burned, but not anymore. There were too many dead and not enough living. Besides, those still alive weren't worried about disease. They would be gone themselves, soon enough. Out of respect or a promise, a husband may bury his wife, or a child his mother, but there were millions, billions, of bodies out there.

She took Peter by surprise. "I hope there's life on other planets," she said. She paused then, again; grew distant, again. She wasn't waiting for a response from Peter. She wasn't listening for anything that might be spoken in this kitchen. Her face had a vague, faraway look. "I would hate to think that all the life in the universe was here on this planet. That would mean that when the last of us dies, when you die, then the universe will be empty."

Peter leaned forward, "Anna, I—"

"If there is no one left to witness the universe's existence, it's just... here."

"I guess so."

"Each day we come closer and closer to that."

Peter leaned back in his chair again and turned away. When he looked at her, he saw too many monsters, too many of his own fears. She was setting those monsters free, giving them sound and voice and physical form.

She was saying aloud all those things that he had tried so hard to keep hidden away, pushed deep in the shadows in back of his mind where he wouldn't have to face them.

He looked toward the door that led to the living room.

Where was the little boy who once lived in this house?

Not dead...

Maybe the family went to go find his grandma and grandpa...

Poor little boy...

The little boy had been happy and safe, born into a sweet, happy world where he was protected from all the bad and all the scary. Then one day there came an evil that his parents could not shield him from. From all around him there came horror and despair and fear. What must it have been like to see the wonder of life through a small child's eyes, then watch it all rot away? What went through his beautiful, trusting mind in his last days?

Peter realized that he was crying. He hadn't thought there had been any tears left in him. He stood and went to the window, looked out at the house across the side yard, then down at the bowl that he had placed in the sink.

Does she wash the dishes? he thought again. *Where does she get her water?*

He tried to hold back his sobs, but couldn't. Anna came up behind him, wrapped her arms around his waist and held onto him.

It felt good to have someone hold him. Yes... A warm, caring person was holding him, touching him. He cried openly now, for the little boy, for all that had happened, for the woman who was comforting him. In the middle of all this sickness and death, he had found Anna, and all the emotions that he had held back all these months burst out. Peter turned and wrapped his arms around this person who cared, who knew what he was going through because she was going through it, too. He could feel that she was crying now, as well. She held him more tightly, buried her face in his shoulder. He squeezed her, pulled her into him and wrapped himself around her as if to swallow up this warm body. He wept into the thick, sweet smell of her hair. How long had it been since he had held another person? How long since he had spoken to another person?

Never again, alone. Never. Never, never. Someone to talk to, to hold on to, to share.

And I will be there for her....

I will be strong for her...

"God, I'm so glad I found you." He barely got the words out, wasn't sure that she could hear him or understand what he had said. Then he heard her muffled cries and she was nodding her head. She rubbed his back and held on as if to never let go. A wash of emotion rushed through him.

Anna pulled back her head, looked up at Peter. Her lips were quivering, her cheeks were streaked with tears. "I don't want to be alone," she said.

"You won't be. Not anymore." Feelings for this woman welled up inside him until he could hardly breathe. He felt dizzy, heady.

But... he didn't even know her... how could he possibly have feelings for her? Could this be some kind of *Last Man and Woman* thing? Would he have felt this way if it had been someone else that he had found in this kitchen?

Confusing thoughts—muddled, confusing thoughts...

Is this another symptom?

Peter tried to push it all away. What he knew for sure was that he felt something when he held her and he had no intention of letting her go. He knew that the two of them had only a few months to live. *How can I be happy?* Yet he was. Somehow, he was. They would live those last months together.

Emotions continued to bubble up inside him. Never, not even before the sickness had stricken the planet, had he felt this way.

With this newfound bliss came newly born hope. He was allowed to believe that maybe, just maybe, the little boy who had once lived in this house might still be alive. And just maybe the doctors and the scientists would come up with the miracle cure that Anna says could not possibly come in time. Maybe some people, maybe the little boy, would live through this.

Just maybe...

Peter moved slowly across the kitchen and sat at the table. He reached across and spoke gentle, loving words, laughed lightly at a response that may have been whispered as if into his ear alone. Sitting back, his arms brushed at the heavy layer of dust that covered the table. The kitchen was gray and dingy, and the dust covered everything. A cup and saucer rested on the table in front of an empty chair, abandoned long ago. The inside of the cup was stained from a remaining swallow of coffee that had been left behind and evaporated away months earlier. The rim of the cup was chipped. Pointing to the cup now, Peter asked his companion if she would like a refill. Looking to the empty chair, he listened to her response, stood and walked over to the counter, talking over his shoulder as he opened the cupboard. There was a single can of peaches, an empty jar of instant iced tea mix, and three packets of Kool-Aid.

Glancing once at the sink, he wondered again whether she washed her dishes or simply tossed them out the kitchen window and into the yard.

Laughing at something Anna said, Peter almost dropped the jar of tea mix that he was taking from the well-stocked cupboard. He smiled as he looked back at her. The more she opened up to him, the more he realized just how wonderful she was. The more he realized just how much he needed her. He would do his best to make her happy in the few months she had left. Together, they would share their joys as well as their fears.

Peter would see that Anna was never alone again.

No one should have to be alone...

Reunions

Introduction

"Reunions" was first published in Necrology Magazine, Tales of Macabre and Horror, a publication tending toward the H.P. Lovecraft type of dark story. Someone suggested that I write an offbeat horror tale, and this little story was the result.

Reunions

Mrs. Johansen held tightly to the handles of the walker and pushed it through the door, following carefully along behind it as she came into the small dining hall. The others were already there, sitting at the one, round table situated in the middle of the room; Mr. Borden, Miss Margaret, Old Mason. They turned about as she came in. Familiar faces from out of the past. Mr. Borden stood and bowed his head in greeting. Mrs. Johansen smiled briefly in response and continued her way to the table.

Old Mason pulled out a chair for her. She stood beside it, shuffled to turn herself around and into position. Her shallow breaths shuddered past aged, trembling lips. She struggled to balance herself, one hand on the walker and the other held in the air above the handle, readying herself to reach for the back of the chair. Old Mason held it firmly in place as she made the move from her walker.

She smiled again; a genuine smile that shed a dozen years from her face and turned her wrinkles into laugh lines. There was life shimmering behind the gleaming green eyes; the only evidence of a strength of spirit that had not diminished, that refused to follow the dead-end path of her now weak and imperfect body. The gentlemen at the table smiled back; Miss Margaret raised one brow and gave her silent welcome.

With Mrs. Johansen's arrival, the group was whole; it was *Oneness*, and they could all feel it. It was warm and satisfying, and the completeness gave each of them a greater sense of awareness, a returned sense of purpose and connection. During their time apart, they had lived lives, experienced adventures, and watched as the galaxy around them continued to spin and the universe continued to expand. All the while, through all the years, within each of the four of them, there had existed a hollow place that was not quite empty, a dark place from which emerged faint echoes of the souls of the others. The long years had passed, and they had survived those years knowing that one day, *this day*, they would be together again and whole.

Mr. Borden served the soup. They took their time. There was no rush. Mr. Borden had rented the hall for the night. They talked as they ate. There were some regrets, and more than a few boasts. Old Mason brought up Miss Margaret's little escapade in Phoenix. It had made the national news. Mrs. Johansen spoke of the grandchildren that she had helped raise after her son had been killed.

Mostly, though, they talked about how it felt to be back together again.

As Mr. Borden cleared away the bowls, Miss Margaret brought coffee in from the kitchen. They relaxed and talked about their plans for the future. Some of the plans were small, some grandiose. There was a building excitement in the air. They would miss one another, as they always did, and that feeling of being apart from one another would lie within them, as it always did; but there was little to be done about that. It was the way of things.

Then it was time.

Little by little, those around the table grew quiet; a heavy somberness lay over the room. Mr. Borden took Mrs. Johansen's left hand; Old Mason took her right. Across the table, Miss Margaret sat tall, with her back straight, her eyes closed and hands gripping tightly to the gentlemen on either side of her.

Mrs. Johansen closed her eyes and slowly lowered her head until her chin rested on her chest. Numbness rose up from somewhere deep within her, spreading out, reaching out to her legs and feet, to her arms and hands, gripping at her fingers as she gripped the fingers of Mr. Borden and Old Mason. She felt a pressure in her heart as she shared her energy with her companions in the circle. The energy of the others rushed back to her, washed over her, plunged into her and pushed the air from her lungs. She threw back her head and gasped suddenly, desperately.

They were One. They were beyond the circle. They were beyond the room, and then beyond the building. They swam the clouds that darkened the evening; they caressed the mountain peaks that rose up around the town; they danced across the stars that were just beginning to show themselves. They were free for the first time in decades and they permitted themselves these few moments to explore the emotions of their release; taking in the world, taking in the space beyond it, absorbing the sensations they were allowed to feel only twice each century.

Then they set about to business.

They began the search.

They found a group of scouts on a camping trip, sitting around a fire and telling tepid ghost stories. They cautiously reached inside each of them, one by one, delicately touching at their life force, delicately caressing the energy surrounding the core of their souls.

They took a day of life from each of them. They took two days from the scoutmaster.

A young man slept in front of his television. He was dreaming that he had won the lottery and was accepting the first check. They took a week of his life. He would die a week sooner, but he would never notice.

They found a lonely old woman who had slipped on the floor in her kitchen as she had been washing her plate and cup at the sink. There was no one to help her. They took her last day.

A man sat hidden away in an alley, huddled beside a dumpster that smelled of rotting lettuce and tomatoes. He was 34 years old, but looked 60. As they took a year from him, he fell back and hit his head. He now had six months left to him and he would spend it in a drunken stupor, stumbling about in abandoned buildings and dirty alleys.

They drew two years of life from a newborn as she drew in her first breath. She would die when she was 74 instead of 76.

They took the last breath of a police officer who had been gunned down on a domestic call.

From a young couple in the throes of passion they took a year each.

A woman, much too young to be a grandmother, lost two months as she watched her young daughter giving birth to her grandson.

They took a week from another woman as she carried her groceries out to her car, exhausted after a long day that had hours yet to go.

Finding a baby that would die in three years, they did not know from what, they took it all. When the proud young parents looked in on the child moments later, their lives came crashing down around them, lives that would not be shortened, lives that would be filled with years of doubt and guilt and grief.

Shadows scurried about in the night. Seconds passed to minutes, and the minutes to hours. They fed throughout the long night, snatching away precious moments of warm existence from the flickering lights of souls lying within every spirit they came upon. As the night slipped into those empty hours before dawn and they finished the feeding, the searchers sought again the circle.

The room was there, the table, the four companions with eyes now empty and without color. The bodies were old and weathered; the bones fragile and muscles worn from long decades of use.

That which had become One now returned to the circle. Slowly, with a sense of trepidation and loss, the One again become four. That which was Mrs. Johansen again realized a sense of self, a sense of individual identity. There was a brief moment of heartrending anguish as she was again the old woman.

She screamed in pain as an explosion of life energy burst from a tiny core within her and struck out to every cell of her body, every fiber of her being. It reached into her brain, into her heart, into her ancient soul, and swept through her decrepit form like fire—burning, scrubbing away the years a second at a time.

The eternal companions remained locked hand in hand throughout what remained of the night.

In the morning, young Mason brought fresh clothes out from the closet. Josie and Maggie went into the women's restroom to clean up and dress as Mason and Bill did the same in the men's restroom. The four of them lingered over a large breakfast of eggs, ham and toast, knowing that once they left, it would be another fifty years before they saw each other again.

Josie brushed back her thick, dark hair and smiled broadly at the others. The life and soul hidden away behind her gleaming green eyes showed a strength of spirit that would not diminish with time. The young men at the table smiled back; Maggie raised one brow, offered a slight smile in return. Then it was time for them to leave.

End

Last Day at Sharp Park

Introduction

In 1962, when I was a little boy, five or six years old, my mom moved us into a rundown converted motel that sat just off a dismal gray beach in one of those small towns south of San Francisco.

My great grandmother stayed with us for a brief time. I don't remember the exact circumstances, but I think she was caring for me while my mother was at work. Mom moved us around a lot back then.

I have several snapshot memories of our time at that ugly motel on that lonely stretch of beach. One is of a day I got off the school bus and found my grandma waiting for me on the bench that faced the ocean. Instead of going inside, we went for a long walk. It was gray and very foggy. I had the feeling that something was wrong, but she never said what that might be. We just walked along the beach, the sound of the waves coming to us through the fog. To this day I remember the stench of rotting seaweed hanging heavy in the salt-laden air.

A number of years later, when I was about 15 years old, I wrote a story about that day. Being that I often see things rather differently than you humans, there may be some slight otherworldly spin on what really happened back then.

Hey, it's my world; I'll make of it what I want.

So... here's a short story written in 1971 by a fifteen year old boy still haunted by that afternoon back when he was six...

Last Day at Sharp Park

The old woman closed the door behind her and stepped off the tiny slab of concrete that served as the porch. The day was cold and wet and gray, and the damp was carried on a dull, chilling wind that seeped into her bones and pushed against her spirit and her will. She walked across the narrow strip of yard and took the wooden steps up the embankment that separated the small, weathered house from the beach and followed the walkway that led back around to the road.

She sat on the bench to wait for Davy. The bench faced the beach, but turning sideways she could look up the road and watch for the small, yellow school bus. It would stop at the intersection and the old woman's grandson would climb out and make the walk to the road's end and the cluster of tiny houses.

The six houses, converted from an old motel, were grouped together on the north side of the narrow road where the road emptied into a little parking lot. The houses were protected from high tides by an eight-foot high manmade embankment that took away whatever ocean view there might once have been. The south side of the narrow road bordered the back of a golf course that ran up the beach for half a mile before turning inland. The bench the old woman sat on was one of several that lined the parking lot that butted up against the beach. The lot was really just the end of the road, widened out enough to allow the few tenants a place to park, and with a little extra room for the occasional beachcomber.

This wasn't one of the more popular beaches. It was off the main tourist routes, not readily accessible, and wasn't particularly inviting. The old woman shifted uncomfortably and looked up the beach.

On top of everything else, it wasn't a very inviting day. The fog was rolling in, turning a cold, damp afternoon even more miserable. She would be glad to get Davy away from here.

There was a time when she had actually liked this place. The sound of the waves, the haunting cry of the birds, the smells born on the sea winds, the brush of the fog on her face and the sensation of sand grinding beneath her feet. She closed her eyes and tried to bring back some of what she must have felt during those first months after arriving.

She meditated; she could hear the hollow roar of the ocean, the lapping sound of the waves, and the screeching of one lonely gull. But these were with them always, were a constant part of their existence, and had become the background noise that dulled all other sounds.

The smells overwhelmed; rotting seaweed, waterlogged debris, thick gray sand that never dried, and the pungent salty reek that dominated everything.

The old woman gave up and opened her eyes. She was probably looking for something that had never really existed to begin with. She turned about to look again at the group of ugly little houses. The fog was growing thicker and the windows of several of the homes had a fuzzy yellow glow. The windows of the nearest house, out of which she had come, were a dull black. She stared at the narrow, faded door.

What a hideous little hovel. It was damp, dark, and smelly with age and an immoral past.

The sound of the school bus stopping at the intersection startled her. She stood and stepped around the bench, rested a hand on it and waited. The fog had grown so thick that she couldn't see it, but the sound of it, and the flashing lights, told her that the bus was there. She heard it pull away. It was some time before she saw the silhouette of a little boy set against the heavy gray mist.

Such a small, vulnerable child; the old woman nearly burst into tears at the sight of him. He was so thin, with wild, light brown hair bleached almost yellow from the sun. He walked awkwardly now, absentmindedly, occasionally glancing at the golf course where the fog sometimes twisted about into strange shapes across the gently rolling slopes. Today, however, it simply rolled over the wet grass and turned everything to shades of gray.

The boy caught sight of the old woman and his face brightened and he ran to her, calling out to her. He threw his arms around her and they hugged. She kissed the top of his head, then turned his head up and kissed his forehead and his cheeks and his nose and gave him a big, grandma kiss on the mouth. She hugged him again, squeezed him to her, then told him they should take a walk along the beach. She told him that she loved walks on the beach.

Davy followed beside her, glancing back once at his house. The windows were dark.

Where was everybody?

They strolled out to where the sand was wet, then turned and began walking up the beach. The fog was now so thick that Davy couldn't see beyond his hands when he held them out in front of him, couldn't see the ocean that was right beside him.

His grandma took his hand and they walked slowly. They were quiet at first, listening to the waves and the roar of the sea. The foam sometimes reached their feet. Grandma didn't seem to mind. Looking up at her, Davy could just make out her face. She was holding it up against the breeze. He turned his own face to the wind now, and felt the dampness against his skin, took in the salt smell and breathed in the wet air.

Davy liked this beach. The outside didn't come here. People didn't come here, like they did other beaches. The only sounds were the ocean's sounds. The only footprints were his footprints. There was the ocean and the sea gulls and him. He liked that.

"Davy," Grandma said suddenly. "We have to leave here soon."

"Where are we going?" Davy felt a twinge of anxiety. He looked back over his shoulder, back towards his house, but it was lost in the mist. "Where's Mommy?"

"Don't worry, sweetie," said Grandma. "Everything is going to be fine."

"Grandma? Where's Mommy?"

Grandma was solemn, silent.

"Grandma?"

"They've found us, honey. We have to leave here."

"Who found us, Grandma?"

Grandma was walking a little faster now, holding tightly to her grandson's hand. Davy, with his tiny, six year old legs, was almost running to keep up.

"Where's Mommy, Grandma?"

"You're going to have to think very clearly now, Davy. You have to be very strong and you have to think very clearly."

Davy had no idea what Grandma was talking about.

"I will, Grandma."

Grandma stopped, pulling Davy up short. She knelt, turned the boy around to face her. "You are going to have to think back now. All right? I need for you to think back to when we first came here. Do you remember when we came to this beach? To this house?"

Of course he remembered. Davy nodded.

"Do you, sweetie? Think very hard."

"Yes." Davy remembered. He and Grandma. And Mommy. And Nicolas and Ben. Nicolas was four, and Ben was three. But not when they moved here. Ben was a baby when they first moved here. Davy wasn't going to school, then. Not yet. He was too young then.

"Do you remember why we came here?"

Davy grew cold. Something was happening in his head.

"Think, Davy."

Davy stared at Grandma. Slowly then, he nodded.

Yes. I remember...

"They're after me. Aren't they, Grandma?"

"That's right, honey." Grandma's face was very stern, but her eyes were soft and warm. Behind her, the rolling fog thinned for a moment and Davy could see the ocean. Then it was gone and the two of them were swallowed up in the cold, wet mist. "Do you remember who is after you?"

"Yes," Davy said flatly.

Grandma took a deep breath and stood. It was returning to him now, after being locked away for three years. Still fragmented, but it would soon come together. She took his hand and they began walking again. The little boy's fingers, so tiny and fragile within her own, were clenching and unclenching, making a little fist inside her palm.

What a terrible, terrible thing she was doing, destroying this little boy's make-believe world. But it was necessary. He had to survive. To survive, he must leave this place.

"We're not going back home?" asked Davy.

"Back to the house? No, Davy. It isn't safe."

"What about my stuff?"

"There is nothing there," Grandma said coldly.

Davy almost stumbled, perplexed. Of course there was. His room was full of stuff. He had his desk, and his shelf full of books, and his dresser full of clothes, and the closet with all his shirts, and the boxes of stuff on the closet shelf, and the toys in the box, and the three games that he kept under his bed. And what about the TV in the living room? And the PlayStation? And the five PlayStation games?

"We have to get Mommy," said Davy.

Grandma stiffened, but kept walking. "No, honey."

"We have to get Mommy, and Nicolas and Ben."

"No, honey."

"But—" Davy was getting dizzy; dizzy and confused.

"There is no reason to go back to the house."

Davy started to cry, but he kept walking.

There was only one small bed in his bedroom...

The games under the bed he would sometimes play with Grandma, but usually he played by himself...

There was only one other bedroom in the house, and that was where Grandma slept...

Grandma picked up little Davy and squeezed him tightly as she walked on. She could feel Davy's sobs as he buried his face in her shoulder. She brushed at his hair with her free hand, and then she too began to cry.

"I want Mommy," he mumbled.

"I know, sweetie." She had to get him away. She had to get him off-planet before they came. With enough of a head start, perhaps it would take another three years to track them down again. The galaxy was a big place, with a million habitable worlds. The Emperor had only so many ships and so many warriors to spare, especially since the horrible war had begun...

When my son murdered his wife and children... all but DahVee—I got little DahVee away...

"Grandma," cried Davy. "I want to go home."

"Me too, Davy." She knew now that he was fully back. He meant *Home*. "I wish we could."

But, of course they could not. Not while Davy's father was still alive.

"Someday," she said, as they vanished into the fog. "Someday, we'll go home."

End

The Light in the Mist

Introduction

Another story born out of a creative writing class. One week, the assignment was to come up with a short story in the vein of a fairy tale. I went out and bought a collection of "Victorian Fairie Tales". So, Victorian it was. I didn't know there was a difference.

That was the influence. Okay, okay... maybe the Victorian Fairie Tale thing ended up as little more than a jumping off point and I went wherever this story ended up taking me. Hey, I got an A out of it...

The Light in the Mist

Galmack gripped the arm of the heavy chair and glared down at the two pathetic creatures kneeling before him. His black claws scratched across the scarred, well-worn wood of the throne arm, instinctively seeking the deep grooves formed there by centuries of his habitual attention. The two shadowy servants sensed his rising anger and threw themselves face down onto the steps at his hooved feet, spread their arms wide and began to whimper.

Galmack smiled unpleasantly. A thin line of spittle ran from the corner of his wide mouth and down his long, pointed chin. A growl began from somewhere deep within his massive, barreled chest and rolled out of him, filling all parts of the dank hall. The guards standing at the door shifted nervously. As the sound faded, Galmack leaned back and let his large, horned head rest against the back of the throne.

"A lack of sincerity," Galmack hissed. There was heat in his whisper, and the two lying prostrate at his feet felt the leathery skin on their backs begin to burn. If they lived beyond this day, there would be much pain, yet but for the barely perceptible twitching of their stubby tails, they did not move. They did not speak.

Their master sighed sorrowfully. The timber in the walls of the great room trembled. He closed his eyes and grew thoughtful.

Galmack's periodic outbursts were necessary, of course, but he tended toward such *unplanned* occurrences when those before him were well beyond breeding age. He could little afford to destroy servants indiscriminately. These two were young, just entering their breeding years. A pity...

His anger rose up within him again, coming up hot in his throat, more because he could not bring himself to kill them than for their ineptitude. His world was growing smaller, and because of that he was forced to endure the very incompetence that was the cause of all his woes.

He stood and took the two steps down to the creatures. Their fear washed over Galmack, warming him, feeding him. His hands reached out involuntarily.

How pleasant it would be. He had only to take their tiny skulls, one in each hand, and squeeze...

Daniel wed his childhood sweetheart and together they moved to the small valley far to the east of the village. They built a three-room house on the northern hillside, and they made this their home. From the doorstep, they could watch the seasons change; the summers were never too hot or too dry, the winters never too harsh. In the spring, the grasses and the trees were all shades of green, the flowers yellow and white and blue. The autumn saw the trees turn orange and brown and red. The man and his wife were happy.

Daniel worked with wood, which he skillfully shaped into the figures of the animals that he saw in the valley. Hanna worked with clay, which she shaped into pots and plates and bowls. On these she painted the images of the flowers that she saw in the meadow below their modest home. The carvings and the pots and plates and bowls they would take to the village and sell at the market. In this way they earned enough for their needs.

Late one Autumn, the man and the woman had a daughter. Sarah was sweet and happy and was a part of the valley. As soon as she was old enough, her days were spent at play outside the front door of their home on the hillside. By her sixth year, the entire valley was her playground; the daylight hours were spent in the woods, the meadow, the grassy slopes, and along the several brooks that meandered through the valley. She made friends with the deer and the rabbits and all the creatures that made the valley their home.

Also living in the valley but seldom seen were the Fairies of the waterfall. When she sat on a particular rock along the left side of the waterfall, and when the sun was just above the trees on the clearest of mornings, Sarah could see the Fairies as they played in the mist. The soft falls would dance and sparkle with life, occasionally reaching out to caress the cheek of the little girl. At this she would laugh, and hold her face against the cool mist and reach her hands into the water. She could sense the purity in the spirits of the Fairies, could feel the joy in their hearts, and now and then she could hear their voices as they laughed and sang.

Sarah was almost ten when a great darkness fell over the valley. It came on a day early in the spring, as she sat on her special rock in the bright, midmorning sun. A shadow fell across the falls and chased the Fairies deep into the water. Sarah turned and looked up at the sky.

There was something not right with this gray.

It was nothing that she could put into words, but she could feel it; there was something very wrong. She knew it. There was something there, something that did not belong, something that did not belong in the valley. There was something that did not belong anywhere. She stood, shivering in the sudden dankness of this strange world that threatened to envelope her. A slate-gray chill began burrowing its way into her. She turned and ran from the waterfall, and by the time she was home, little Sarah was crying.

With the Darkness came gray skies and clouds near black, and rains that lasted for weeks on end. With the Darkness came the swamps and the muddy bogs. With the Darkness, the grasses withered and the wildflowers died, the woods turned barren, the brooks swelled and muddied.

The home of the man and the woman and the little girl was as damp and gloomy as the unending season of gray that held the valley. It was difficult for Daniel to find wood dry enough to burn to keep them warm. He could find no wood suitable for carving. Hanna could find no clay suitable for making pots and plates and bowls. With nothing to trade, there was nothing with which to earn their keep. When their food ran out, the family lived on what they could find in the valley or managed to grow in the saturated earth of their small garden.

Spring left and summer came, and still the skies did not clear. There were no dry days. The gray was the gray that pulled down the soul, that dragged at the spirit and the heart. It grew more difficult each day for Daniel to force himself out of the house to search for food and kindling. Each day, it was the sight of little Sarah, sad and cold and hungry, that sent him out. Each day, he returned with little to eat and he was all the more weary for the day spent in search of what little could be found.

During these wanderings, Daniel would sometimes come upon the waterfall where his daughter had spent so many hours in better times. When finding himself there, he would often stop to rest, sometimes for several hours. He would sit on Sarah's special rock and watch the water work its way down the craggy hillside. Its magic no longer showed itself, but Daniel could feel a purity within the falls and it seemed to him the mist would sometimes wash just a little of the darkness from his heart and allow him to continue for one more day.

Sarah never came to the waterfall; not since the coming of the Darkness. She seldom left the house, and then went only as far as the garden. There she would toil in the muddy earth, digging for the few carrots and potatoes they managed to grow.

The summer was two-thirds gone and there was no sign that the gray was going to leave. Daniel had traveled to the far end of the valley this day and was on his way back to Hanna and little Sarah when he decided to stop again at the waterfall. It was late, but it wasn't far out of the way, and a few moments there would return him home in better spirits.

As he neared the falls, Daniel heard sounds—animal sounds, but unlike anything that he had heard before in the valley. These were sounds unfamiliar and yet known, for these were the sounds of a little boy's night terrors.

He approached cautiously, haunted by the stories that he had heard as a child and the visions those stories had left behind.

There they were—at his little girl's waterfall. Galmack's creatures.

He is here...

Daniel watched from his hiding place as the servants of Galmack scrambled across and about the falls, searching, searching... squealing grotesquely as they groped beneath the water with their bony-fingered hands and pulled out the terrified Fairies one by one, stuffing them into large bags as black as the dark, empty eyes of the evil creatures that held them. The goblins shrieked with joy each time they had one of the little Fairies in hand, crying out in fear. The little sparks of life would squirm and struggle, fighting to get away, occasionally breaking loose and rushing back into the water. More often they did not get away and were stuffed into the black bags.

The gray sky gave way to full night before the creatures were through. There were no more Fairies in the waterfall. The goblins scurried away, eager to be far from the water and more eager yet to return their newly acquired treasure to their Lord.

Not until they were long out of sight and hearing did Daniel dare to come out of hiding and rush home.

"What will we do?" asked Hanna. "We'll have to leave the valley."

"We can't stay here," Daniel agreed. It was late in the night, but they had not yet gone to bed. They could not sleep. They sat at the small table, a single candle flickering between them.

Hanna and little Sarah had been worried when Daniel had not returned home by nightfall. They were relieved to see

202 David R. Beshears

him, only to be troubled once again when he told them of what he had witnessed at the waterfall. Sarah began to cry and wanted to hurry back to the waterfall. Daniel held her in his arms until the sobbing stopped. Together then, Daniel and Hanna told their daughter of Galmack, the evil king of a lost and wicked race, long ago driven from this land and thought forever gone. He could not live in the world of bright sunshine and was repulsed by kindness and good. He could only exist in the gray gloom and thrived on all that was bad, fed on sadness and fear.

Now he had returned, and was reshaping this valley to be his home, coloring it to his need for shadow and dark.

With thoughts and images such as these, Sarah had fallen silent before the faint warmth of the fireplace, staring into the glow of the small fire that Daniel had managed to keep going. She had finally fallen into a fitful sleep and Daniel carried her to bed.

They would have to leave the valley. Perhaps they would move back to the village. Perhaps they would find another valley. Wherever they went, it would not be home. It would not be here.

Galmack has taken our valley from us.

In the morning, Daniel woke to a scratching knock on their door. When he opened it, he saw three small, ugly creatures standing on the front stoop. They were a third his height, naked and damp, with frog-like features not unlike the things that he had seen at the waterfall the day before.

More of Galmack's servants...

Daniel reached quickly for the wooden staff that he kept beside the door.

"Away, you!" He held the staff before him.

The creatures backed away quickly, out of reach of the long staff and several paces beyond. The man came outside the house, emboldened now, out into the open and where he could fight if need be, and held his weapon at the ready.

"Let my family be!"

At this, one of the three stepped forward and spoke. It was not in any language that Daniel could understand or had ever heard. He was taken slightly aback at the softness of the voice; it was not harsh or wicked or threatening, but rather gentle and kind. Nor were the words in any way ugly, despite the hideous appearance of the creature that spoke them. When it had finished its few short sentences, the thing stepped back, and its companions nodded urgently, their heavy heads bobbing up and down with some sense of desperation.

Maybe these weren't servants of Galmack, then, but more of his victims.

"I can't help you," he said. "Leave us alone." What was he supposed to do for them? He couldn't help them; he could barely keep his own family alive. Besides, he was soon going to take his family out of the valley.

The creatures didn't leave. They stood, heads now still, and watched the man as he slowly lowered the staff to his side. They made no effort to come nearer, yet showed no inclination to return whence they had come.

"Please," Daniel pleaded, "we can do nothing for you. I can offer you neither protection, nor food. We grow hungry ourselves. What little food we would give to you would come from the mouth of my little Sarah. This I will not do."

At that last, all three of the creatures jumped forward, speaking hurriedly, frantically, desperately. Daniel quickly brought his staff again to bear, certain that they were about to attack, that something he had said had either offended them or in some other way angered them.

"Go! Go! Leave us!" He pushed his staff forward, in the direction of the creatures, to show that he meant what he said to be done.

It was several moments more before the three were able to regain their calm. A sadness hovered about them now, strong enough that the man could feel it. He knew that he could not give in to it, that if he showed any further sign of weakness, he would never get them to leave.

He stood his ground. "Leave now," he demanded.

With this they turned about and started slowly along the muddy path that led down the hillside from the house. Daniel watched them until they were out of sight, then turned and went into the house.

Hanna waited for him there, having watched it all from the window beside the door. Daniel returned the staff to its place and put his arms around his wife. As he held her, their daughter came into the room and stood sleepily before them.

"Where are the Fairies?" she asked.

"These were not Fairies," said Daniel.

"I heard them."

The mother knelt before little Sarah, gave her a hug, brushed back her hair and kissed her forehead. "You were having a dream, Sarah."

"I was awake. I heard them."

Hanna stood and turned to her husband. Daniel shook his head uncertainly. He knew that no one could speak the language of the Fairies, but he knew also that his daughter had a special relationship with them, that she could sometimes hear them and understand them; not just with her ears but with her heart.

What if these three creatures were Fairies, thought Daniel, but somehow bedeviled?

"Did you understand what they were trying to say?" he asked.

She nodded. "Something bad has been done to them."

"Yes?"

"They want me to help them."

"What would they have you do, Sarah," asked Hanna doubtfully, "that Fairies could not do for themselves?"

"I do not know," Sarah said. Her voice was quivering. She was coming full awake now, and the realization of what was happening was descending upon her. When she spoke again, the words did not sound like the words of a little girl. It was still Sarah, their sweet daughter, but she now carried a knowledge and a burden far beyond her ten years. "A spell has been laid upon them, but it is not yet finished. When it is, the darkness that has fallen upon our valley will be here forever."

"Sarah?" Hanna was growing frightened, not just for the valley, but for her little girl. "You can stop this?"

"They want me to release them from the spell before it is completed; and then the darkness on the valley will also be gone."

Daniel knew it all to be true; this and more. He could take Sarah's words and place them beside what he knew of Galmack...

Galmack had placed a curse upon three of the Fairies that he had taken from the waterfall. Yes. It would be like Galmack to make the spell all the more cruel by offering them an escape from their affliction. They had come here for help. Daniel had turned them away, as Galmack must have known he would.

Daniel held his daughter in his arms. "I'll find them," he said. "I will bring them back." He put on his hat and coat, took his staff in hand, and left.

He returned that evening, cold and hungry and alone. He emptied his pockets of the few nuts and berries and roots that he had found while searching for the Fairies. As they ate he told him of his day. He had searched the hillside, the barren woods, the swampy meadows, the brooks, and the waterfall. There had been no sign of them. The rains had washed away what tracks they may have left behind. He would go out again tomorrow.

Daniel searched for the Fairies all the next day, and the next, and the day after that. Hanna looked for them as well, and Sarah searched all the places she thought they might be. All the while, the Darkness that lay over the valley grew stronger and heavier. There was less and less to eat, and the man, the woman and the little girl grew pale and thin and weak. Eventually, all of what little food that was found was given to Sarah. Most days, Daniel and Hanna did without.

By the beginning of autumn, Hanna was too weak to leave the house. It was too much for her even to get out of bed. Daniel and their little Sarah continued to look for the Fairies.

Then, one morning, Daniel woke and found that he also was too weak to get out of bed.

Sarah continued on alone. Almost too feeble now to travel the winding path, she returned to the waterfall. She often came here first, early in the morning, before beginning her day's search. She would sit and watch the darkened water, remembering the way it was in happier times, the way it would sparkle with Fairie life, the way it would reach out to her and touch her cheek and make her laugh.

On this day she sat on her special rock, as always, along the left side of the falls, wrapped her arms around her knees, and stared into the water as it splashed down the rocks and into the small pool below. As always now, the day was gray and wet, and left Sarah chilled in spirit and body. There was little left in the falls now to wash away the growing darkness that surrounded her heart. She rested her head on her knees. She felt a tingling inside her as the falls struggled to cleanse her, to restore some sense of light and hope to her. That faded away, and then there was nothing.

Sarah reached a hand out and touched the water, too weak to do much else. She would not be leaving here again. Her last day would be spent beside the waterfall that had been the greatest joy of her life. She began to cry. Her tears ran down her cheeks and onto the wet rock.

In the gray surrounding the waterfall, a faint shimmer shown in the mist above the rock upon which her tears had fallen. It was barely visible, and it looked to fade into and out of existence. After several moments, the gentle sparkling of light spread up to wash across the little girl's wet cheeks.

This appeared to Sarah as the memories of joys forever lost, and she continued to weep. The shimmering light, still so faint that it could barely be seen, danced in the mist, reaching out toward the falls themselves. For a moment, Sarah thought she saw something, and she raised her head enough to look more closely. The image vanished.

The mist grew steadily brighter.

There it is again.

Sarah began sobbing silently, for hidden there deep within the waterfall, just visible, were three hideous little creatures. Three ugly, piteous little beings sat on a ledge within the waterfall, clutching to each other and looking despondently out beyond the falls.

She sobbed openly, now. She had found them. At last, she had found them, but she was too near death to help them. Sarah carefully laid down upon the rock, reaching a shaky hand out in the direction of the falls.

She closed her eyes and surrendered to sleep.

From within the waterfall, the creatures saw Sarah lying on her special rock and realized that she had seen them. They also began to weep. They wept with joy, for though they too were near death and were too weak to move beyond the ledge, their Sarah had come looking for them. They held to each other all the more tightly, and also closed their eyes.

Their tears reached the pool below and rose again with the mist. The mist swelled and rose higher, until it found the little girl, her face damp with her own final tears, tears that she had shed for the three Fairies held within the spell. The mist reached out and caressed Sarah's face. The water glimmered and sparkled, and the shimmering light began to spread, brighter now. Sarah's eyes opened, and she now found that she had enough strength to sit up, though slowly. She watched as the light within the mist and the water reached into the falls and touched the three creatures hidden within. Their eyes opened. Still holding one another, they stood up unsteadily and let the water rush over them. The falls ran clearer and brighter; the three creatures began to shimmer as well, then paled to bright, misty orbs.

Sarah began to laugh. She held her hands out before her to let the bright, clear water run through her fingers. Her face glowed with the cool, wet mist and the tears that ran freely down her cheeks.

The sky directly overhead began to clear, turning a pale blue, then a deep, bright blue. The sun shone through and the woods around the waterfall were suddenly streaked with bright yellow sunlight. The air around the waterfall began to sparkle with the dancing light of Fairies.

The others were returning home, rushing home, freed now from their imprisonment by the servants of Galmack. They darted about the falls, into the mist and out, circling around Sarah, around and around, singing out their joy and their affection. Sarah laughed and sang with them. She sat there on the rock, smiling and giggling, too weak to stand or walk. One by one, the Fairies came to her, kissed her lightly on the cheek, and entered the waterfall. When the last had returned, the waterfall of the Fairies sparkled as clear and bright as it had before the coming of the great Darkness.

The shimmering light of the waterfall reached out across the valley. It reached the home of Daniel and Hanna and little Sarah. It reached further, beyond the valley, to the great hall deep in the mountain that was the dark lair of Galmack. He roared out in anger and the mountain shook. The great thunderclap shattered across the sky and cleared away the last of darkness.

Daniel found Sarah asleep on the rock beside the waterfall. He carefully lifted her in his arms, carried her home and put her to bed. There she slept until late the next morning, dreaming of warm sunshine, wildflowers and Fairies.

End

Room

Introduction

At the end of class late one Tuesday evening, our creative writing teacher gave us an assignment that was to be handed in on Thursday. We were to write a "white room" story. This is one in which there is usually only a single, minimal set, very few if any objects, and the characters interact primarily with one another.

I had been mulling over a scene in my mind for a larger story I was thinking about writing (never did), and I thought it might fit the requirements for the assignment. Since we only had two days, I decided to go with it. In the end, it came fairly close to what the teacher wanted, though there were a few things in the room (unseen overhead light, door, walls), and I did cut away to another set and set of characters at one point. It was well received in class, and I did get another A out of it.

I ran across the story years later, along with my notes for the novel I had been thinking about at the time. You have a read and you tell me whether or not this looks more like a scene from a low-budget sci-fi B movie...

Room

The door closed slowly behind him, coming to rest in its jam with a heavy, hollow sound. The darkness swept up and enveloped him, washed over him, and gripped at his chest. He stood motionless, clutching at the cloth bag that held the few possessions they had allowed him.

Paul Mendel sensed that he was not alone, and after a few moments he thought that he could hear breathing. The soft sound came from no direction in particular and from all directions at once. He waited, and as his eyes adjusted there was a lessening of the dark some distance directly ahead of him. He stepped towards it.

The sounds remained unchanged. He walked slowly, and as he drew nearer, Paul could see a circle of light some ten feet across forming a luminescent, ethereal cylinder of light that spanned floor to ceiling. A few more steps and he was standing at its edge, the gray coveralls and the open-toed sandals that he wore glowing faintly.

He stepped into the light, and when nothing happened he let out a long breath and moved into the center of the circle. Above him, the light shimmered as an indistinct haze. Around him, the world beyond the circle was a great, black shadow reaching into the unknown; a shadow that held the faint sounds of life, though what that life was he did not yet know.

"It's not as empty as it feels." It was a woman's voice, coming from somewhere in the dark. She was nearby but safely hidden.

"It doesn't feel empty at all," said Paul, looking in the direction of the voice. He spoke with a calmness that he didn't really feel.

"I sometimes think of it as a populated void," she said.

"You don't see many of those."

"Yeah, well, this place is full of contradictions." There was a deliberate softness to the voice, as if she was afraid the world around her might shatter if she wasn't careful. "It's intentional."

"Would you mind? I'd feel more comfortable if I could see you."

A young woman stepped into view, stopping just at the perimeter of light. She was slim in her own gray coveralls. She wore her dark hair pulled back into a long ponytail. Her hands were stuffed into her pockets. She looked to be in her twenties, and to all appearances she was a fellow prisoner. She gave a slight nod. "I'm Robin Palmer."

"Paul Mendel." There was an uncomfortable silence. "How many are we?"

"You make six."

"Quiet bunch. Where are the others?"

"Here. There is nowhere else." She turned, indicated that he should follow. "You interrupted our sleep period."

She disappeared from view. Paul had to hurry after her, following the sound of her footsteps. He allowed himself to be led away from the light, taking short, cautious, yet quick steps. Robin seemed not to be bothered at all by the fact that they were effectively blind. She knew exactly where she was going, and when she got there she came to a sudden stop.

"This is your private area," she said. "You can leave your bag here. No one will bother it."

Paul could sense a mass in front of them, but he could see nothing. Reaching out, he came into contact with a wall. It was cool, smooth, and when he ran his hand some short distance to one side, sensed a very slight inward curve.

"You'll find a mat on the floor; a blanket and pillow," said the woman.

He realized that she was about to move away, so he dropped his bag, reached out and put a hand on Robin Palmer's shoulder. She tensed slightly, but didn't pull away. After ten steps, they were back to the circle of light. Robin turned thirty degrees to the left and took Paul back into the dark. Ten more steps and she stopped.

"This is the food dispenser," she said matter-of-factly, and pulled his hand off her shoulder.

They were again at the wall, and it had the same slight curve. He realized then that the room was round. Paul found a small opening in the wall about waist high. The compartment inside was filled with soft, fleshy balls the size of large onions. Holding one to his nose, it smelled vaguely of avocado.

"Are they any good?" he asked.

"Edible," she shrugged. "We call them ration fruit, for lack of any better name. Not much flavor, I guess, but they keep us healthy. The bin is always full. You'll find a water fountain set into the wall beside the bin."

Paul heard shuffling in the dark. Some of the others were awake and moving about. This brought an important question to mind.

"Where do you go to the bathroom?"

"There's a cubicle set into the wall on the other side of the room, directly opposite us. Do you want me to show you?"

"The question was for future reference."

"Well that's it, then; the full tour."

"Do they ever turn on the lights?"

"I don't know that there are any lights."

"Except for that light in the middle of the room."

"We call that the Plaza," said Robin. "Central meeting place. As you should have figured out, the areas beyond the Plaza are for the most part divided into our private living areas.

"Regarding privacy, Mr. Mendel, there are two rules. You should get along fine with the rest of us if you follow them. Rule one: Keep the noise down. Rule two: When you move about, stay away from the walls. Walk to the center of the room, turn and go directly to where you need to go. This keeps you from walking through our individual quarters. If you object to either of these rules, make your objections known during a general meeting. Rules are made, changed or discarded by majority vote. It is also suggested, though not required, that you follow the schedule that has been established. Everything sound all right with you?"

"That depends on the schedule."

Robin had expected a simple affirmative. She responded to his comment calmly enough, however. "We have an eight hour sleep period and we meet for meals three times a day.

We have an exercise period mid-morning, and a recreation period mid-afternoon. There is sometimes a storytelling in the evening."

"Sounds interesting."

"Yes," she said, flatly. "The Major is our clock. He's as close to a timepiece as we have in here. Not everyone gets involved in every activity, and you don't have to attend on a daily basis, but it would keep you busy. With a new arrival in town, attendance should be high at today's activities."

"If this is your sleep period, it may take me a while to get adjusted to the schedule. It's late afternoon outside."

"As I said, following the schedule is voluntary."

"I'll do my best, Miss Palmer."

Paul Mendel sat at the edge of the Plaza, his legs crossed and slowly growing numb. His five new companions sat with him, finishing their breakfast of ration fruit. Robin had introduced each of them, and each had said a few words about who they were and where they came from. They stared openly at him now, waiting for him to say something about himself. He swallowed the last of his breakfast and glanced about cautiously at the circle of faces. It was a strange mix of people.

In addition to himself and Robin Palmer, there was an army intelligence officer, a college professor, a big city police detective, and a retired government employee.

"I had a wife before the war," he began. "I had two kids. I had a house and a station wagon and a cute little sports car. Then the war came. We escaped into the mountains, and eventually joined up with the Resistance. My wife was killed a year ago, my kids not long after. Then, four or five weeks back, we were overrun by the Kraandar. The few of us who survived the attack were scattered. I've been on my own ever since. I was captured two days ago. Here I am. Wherever *here* is."

"Montana," said Professor Vandover.

"Northern Arizona," said Major Mendosa.

"What line of work were you in, son?" asked Miss Bailey. Ruth Bailey was 62, had retired from state government work a year before the war broke out. In the first week of the conflict she had lost her sister and brother-in-law, and their kids. They had been her family. A lot of people knew an awful lot about losing family.

"My wife and I had an antique furniture store," said Paul. "We looked for items that hadn't been well cared for. We'd get a good price, then repair and refinish, bring them back to life, then put 'em out front for sale."

"That's very sweet," said Miss Bailey. "You and your wife worked together, and at something meaningful; something with purpose."

"We liked what we did. And it provided us as much as we needed."

"How sweet," said Miss Bailey again.

"Sweet," grunted Major Mendosa. "Give us news of the war, Mr. Mendel."

"We're not making it easy for them, Major."

"What the hell does that mean?"

"I'm sorry if I sound vague, but it means just that. We're making it difficult for them to win."

"If you plan to lose, Mendel, you'll never win. Are you a loser, Mendel?" There was the look of growing distaste on the Major's face. He appeared about to spit, as if trying to rid himself of the awful flavor of something rotten that he'd just bitten into. He was clearly not much impressed with the newcomer.

"That's fine for the troops, Major," said Paul, "but I'm afraid that, barring an act of a higher power, we *will* lose. I don't like it, I'm not taking it very well, but I'm not blind to it, either."

Major Mendosa turned away from Paul in an obvious dismissal, shook his head and stared at the floor in front of him, "We couldn't get someone in here with a trained eye? Someone with the background to truly understand the situation outside?"

"Paul's assessment is probably fairly accurate," said Carl. Carl Josephsen was in his late thirties, had thick, bushy hair and a narrow face that held the look of constant contemplation. He had been a police detective before the war and had the calm air of quiet authority.

The Major growled now at Carl. "Yes, we all know your thoughts, Josephsen."

"As we all know yours, Major."

"Please," said Miss Bailey. "Must we always argue amongst ourselves?"

"Best he knows where we all stand," said the Major, though he grumbled under his breath now. Being surly with Miss Bailey apparently made him uncomfortable.

"That can be done without resorting to personal attacks, can it not?" she asked.

"Of course it can, Miss Bailey," said Professor Vandover. The professor was a tall, thin, sixtyish black man, just beginning to gray at the temples. "I believe the Major may be having difficulty restraining his frustration."

"I can speak for myself, Vandover," said Major Mendoza.

"No doubt."

The Plaza was empty but for Paul Mendel and Robin Palmer. Paul smiled and Robin shrugged uneasily.

"Lively," said Paul.

"It gets that way, sometimes," Robin said, shrugging it off. "The Major is all Army Intelligence. I think he feels cheated at having a motley group like us for a command."

"I didn't get the feeling that he was in charge."

Robin laughed, then leaned closer, "Which only adds to his distress."

This was first sign that Robin Palmer was capable of simple pleasant conversation. She was visibly different than she had been in the morning. She was more relaxed around him, now.

"I haven't heard much about you, Robin. How'd you end up in here?"

"Not much to it. I had just picked up my bachelor's, and was starting graduate studies. And the whole world turned upside down. Graduate studies were over."

"There's got to be more to it than it."

"The Professor and I were captured together."

"You and Vandover?"

"There were eight of us at his house when they took us. His wife was killed, and a couple of my friends. He and I ended up here; alone at first. A few weeks later, Miss Bailey was brought in."

Paul looked up at the ceiling, into the light. There was nothing to see but the misty glare.

"How do they treat prisoners?"

Robin shrugged, "We're on our own. The Professor says they're studying us. The Major believes it's more sinister than that."

"What do you think?"

"They're watching us. They're always watching us."

Professor Vandover was sitting alone in the Plaza when Paul came in, several ration fruit in hand.

"Hello, Professor."

"Good morning, Mr. Mendel."

"Paul. Paul is fine." Paul sat beside him. "I wish they would supply us with a few chairs."

"Furniture has been requested, but not provided."

"Yeah? How do you make requests?"

"Young Miss Palmer voices our desires in the general direction of the light above us."

Paul could swear he saw the beginnings of a smile on the Professor's face. He looked up into the light, wondering if, as Robin suggested, they were always watching.

"Does it ever work? Asking the light?"

This time Professor Vandover did manage a smile, if only for a moment. "Not as yet."

Paul held out a ration fruit to the Professor. Vandover slowly shook his head. "No thank you, Mr. Mendel. I will wait for the others."

Paul took another bite of the one that he was eating.

Paul mapped out the room over the next several days. First he calculated the length of his average step. Once he was convinced that he could rely on this average, he went to work. He paced the distance from the wall of his quarters area inward to the center of the Plaza. He did this going both directions, several times. His shortest calculation was within one and a half feet of his longest calculation. He took the average—thirty-five feet.

He performed the same process to the food dispenser, then to the toilet and shower. The distance to each, from the center of the Plaza, was thirty-five feet.

Paul wasn't much for mathematics, so he went with the clock picture. He figured that if his quarters lay at 12 o'clock, then the food dispenser was somewhere near 4 o'clock and the toilet was at 10. He did know enough math to calculate that if this was a circle, and the radius was 35 feet, then the circumference would be a little over 220 feet. He decided to test his math.

Paul waited until the others were in the Plaza. Starting from his quarters, he began a clockwise walk along the wall. He came first to Professor Vandover's quarters. He couldn't actually see anything, but he found the mat at about where he guessed it would be from the direction of the Professor's comings and goings from the Plaza, at just past the 1 on the clock.

Next was the Major's quarters, at almost 3 o'clock. At the 4, Paul found the food dispenser. He found Miss Bailey's quarters at 6 o'clock and Robin's at just past 7. Between 8 and 9, he found the solid door that he had first come through. At 10 was the toilet with the shower stall. Carl Josephsen's quarters were at 11 o'clock. Back at 12, and at about the 220 foot circumference that he had estimated, he was back at his own quarters.

The others had of course known what he was up to, and upon his return to the Plaza had voiced their objections and feigned outrage at his plodding through private quarters, but he sensed it was obligatory fury. They certainly must have expected the new arrival to explore his prison cell, and they hadn't tried to stop him during his exploration. Once he had completed his search, they had dutifully scolded him for his offense and then had dropped the matter. He would not be going through their private areas again.

Paul could not reach the top of the wall. When he asked Carl about it, he was told that some weeks back Robin had stood on his shoulders, and she had not found the top of the wall. This would put the height of the room, at the outer edge, at somewhere beyond 12 feet, perhaps much more. The light above the Plaza was certainly much higher than 12 feet.

The walls and floor felt like metal; cool but not cold to the touch. Inside the food dispenser, Paul could feel the joint that formed the small access from which the ration fruit came. Even if he could manage to pry it open, which he doubted, it was barely wide enough for his hand, just large enough for the ration fruit.

The toilet cubicle, with the overhead shower nozzle, showed nothing in the way of an opportunity.

Paul saw three areas for further research.

First, with the help of the others, he could continue to search for the ceiling. Being as out of reach as it appeared to be, perhaps it was more vulnerable, and perhaps there was a way through.

A second area of further research was the door that he had come in through. The door itself was impenetrable, but if Paul was waiting nearby when someone new was brought in, he could try and make a fight of it. He wasn't hopeful. He couldn't spend all his time waiting by the door, and if he did happen to be there when it was opened, he would be facing jailors who would no doubt be on their guard. There also remained the question as to just what to do if he did manage get past these first guards.

A third possibility was to find a way to have his captors take him out of the room of their own accord. This option, he would have to think on...

"Mr. Mendel?"

Paul turned at the sound. He was standing vigilantly beside the door. "Yes?"

"It's Carl Josephsen."

Paul could just sense a figure in the dark. He heard the faint sound of the police detective's sandals on the floor. Back in the middle of the room, he heard the others talking as they sat about in the Plaza.

"Call me Paul."

"I thought you might be here, Paul." Josephsen stopped. Very little of the light from the Plaza went beyond the Plaza itself, but Paul found that as time passed, his eyes grew more acute to subtle shades of dark, and as some little light did reach out from the center of the room, it was not totally black in the cell. There was light. Paul could in some sense see Josephsen standing beside him. Once he had the man's position, he turned back to the door.

"As good a place as any to idle away the time."

"Of course. Most of us have spent time here. I spent weeks here. Just waiting... I'm not sure what I would have done if the door had actually opened—probably would have jumped back and hid in the dark."

"Can you see everything in here when the light from outside shines in? Can you see the ceiling?"

"Afraid not. You can't tell when you're brought in, Paul, but the moment the door opens, the light in the hall outside goes real dim. From in here, if you're in the right place at the right time, you can make out the silhouette of someone standing in the door, but that's about it."

Paul looked up at the ceiling. It was dark everywhere, but it was darkest up there. If it was totally black anywhere, it was totally black up there.

"Has anyone actually been here at the door when it opened?" he asked.

"Not this near, no."

"Has it ever opened except to let in a new prisoner?"

"Not that I know of." Carl turned at the sound of the Major's raised voice in the Plaza. "Someone has the Major ticked off," he said lightly. Paul sensed the smile on Carl's face. He smiled in return.

"That doesn't take much doing."

"None at all," said Carl. "But then, I guess if we didn't have the Major here, we'd have to make one."

"Suppose so," said Paul. He was about to ask another question that suddenly occurred to him, when he realized that he couldn't remember what it was. It was there, right on the tip of his tongue, and then it was gone.

That's weird...

He felt a strange tingling in his stomach. He thought he heard Carl take in a sharp breath. The voices in the Plaza stopped. Silence closed in from the dark.

The moment passed. It lasted only few seconds, then Miss Bailey was chiding the Major. The Major groaned. Carl, at arm's length in the dark, breathed noisily through his nose.

"Probably right," said Paul.

"People like the Major keep the adrenaline flowing in an otherwise peaceful world." His sandals scratched across the floor, "I'm going to head back. Miss Bailey has promised a storytelling."

"I was just a young thing," said Miss Bailey. "I had been to the Spring Dance, and was on my way home. I stopped in the park and thought I'd sit in the gazebo and enjoy the warm evening for a few minutes."

Miss Bailey had a spark in her eye, as if she was telling the group of something naughty that she had done. Paul found the woman to be quite endearing.

"The gas street lamps that lined the park gave the night a strange, yellowing glow, plenty bright enough to see young Cornelius Smythe approaching." She grinned and nodded knowingly. "I could see the look in his eye beneath the brim of his hat."

Just how old is dear old Miss Bailey?

"The young man took the steps up into the gazebo as sweet as you please, tipped his hat in a gentlemanly way and asked if he might sit beside me a while."

"So what'd you say?" asked Robin with a grin.

"Why, I didn't know what to say. Sit down beside me? Unchaperoned?" Miss Bailey slowly leaned forward, grinned sheepishly, and snickered. "I said yes."

Paul wasn't quite sure at first, but as dear Miss Bailey continued her story, it became more and more evident that the tale she told came from somewhere out of the distant past, far too distant for the woman to have experienced the events herself.

What was unsettling was that she was clearly speaking as if from personal experience and that she was just as clearly expecting everyone to take her story as fact.

Maybe she was merely embellishing an actual event by wrapping it in antiquity.

Perhaps that was what expected from the storytellings. The others didn't seem bothered. They simply took the tale at face value and appreciated the diversion.

Paul wondered why it bothered him so much...

As she went on with her story, Miss Bailey seemed to fall deeper and deeper into the atmosphere of the time. Her words, her tone, the detail in clothing and objects, and the culture and social norms, all spoke of a time long before the world that Paul had come from.

He was glad when she finished her story.

The others in the group had thoroughly enjoyed it. They excitedly asked her questions and she eagerly responded. It all made sense to them. It began to make sense to him.

But it was all wrong.

The room was very large and was filled with row after row of occupied beds of cool metal... humans, all quite old, completely unaware, each being fed intravenously, each with a narrow metal band around the head.

A Kraandar was walking slowly down one of the aisles within the rows of beds. He was of the upper class, and faintly resembled a giant, very overweight grasshopper standing on its hind legs. He stopped at one of the tables and began a cursory examination of the human that was laying there, used its more dexterous upper hands to adjust the equipment.

Another Kraandar came into the room pushing a narrow gurney, upon which slept an old woman. Her thinning hair was brittle and nearly colorless, her skin pale and flaky.

The first Kraandar turned at the sound. It spoke in the sharp, brittle tone of the upper class—the words sounding as if they might shatter in the warm air. "Subject from 13C?" The question was more of a statement. "It is being moved to Room 4A."

The second Kraandar responded acknowledgement in the humble voice of its lower class status, then began to push the gurney up to the head of the fourth row.

Paul heard the door to their cell open and a moment later close. He had been standing near the ration dispenser, and there had been no way for him to get across the room in time.

He found Robin standing in the darkness with a young woman. The new arrival was dressed in the same style of overalls as every prisoner, wore the same flat sandals. She had long, thick brown hair that she wore pulled back into a ponytail.

"Paul," said Robin, sliding to one side as he approached. "This is Carol, recently arrived."

"Good morning," said Paul, and he reached out a hand. He added questioningly, "Morning?"

"Close enough," said Carol. They shook hands. "What is this place?"

"Good question." Paul turned and the three of them started back to the center of the room. "Just got here, then?"

"Yes," she said, following Robin and Paul toward the Plaza. "They brought me in today."

End